THE ORDER
TRILOGY

Book 1: Chacra

SUNDARESH

INDIA • SINGAPORE • MALAYSIA

PROLOGUE

As the call of the wild accentuated the wilderness of the situation he was now placed in, each roar, each echo, was super-amplified to his ears. As he lay on the ground, staring up at the world that he was going to exit, asphyxiation clouded his belief in himself. A sense of foreboding crept over him as he now remembered his life's greatest purpose.

The scroll.

That was it, the entire reason for his existence. His sole reason for ending up here is in Africa. His reason for transcendence. His reason for righteousness.

After a few moments of his childhood whizzed by, he began to feel the toxin setting in his body. The dastardly trap had ended with a bullet to his chest, paralyzing his chest down. Slowly but surely, he felt his life ebb away.

As he fell, his last thought was of the scroll. He knew it was safe, as he had himself buried it in the most secure place that their organization could offer. The secret was safe.

Unfortunately, he was dead wrong.

ॐ ✦ ☙

The lights blazed on as the door slowly revolved, allowing access to the formidable individual now passing its threshold. A reception stood, discreetly tucked away into the corner. On its front, a plaque read: RAW. Research and Analysis Wing.

The man slowly lifted his eyes to the lift, placing his on the iris scanner, which flashed green. The lift slowly opened up to let the Director General of Intelligence at RAW in. His name was Sunil Chabbria.

As he walked into his super modern lab, his assistant Trix ran to him with a printout in hand. Breathless, she handed over the printout. As the contents of the letter came into focus for Sunil, a wave of fear washed over him.

'what happened?' he asked, with a hint of anger.

'Our man is not responding. This was from the African branch contacts. A fresh leak of evidence has now been spotted,' Trix said matter-of-factly.

'So?' Sunil asked, exasperated.

'So, we have a problem. One that might get out of hand if not solved quickly. This is a code red situation.'

'The world is at stake.'

CHAPTER 1

Peru was once the heart of the world. The heartbeat that united the South Americans. The nerve center of world art. And at its core, on the Eastern Cordillera stood the reason for its pride.

Machu Picchu.

The city of the Incas is a true wonder of civilization and, most importantly, the abode of Viracocha. The ancients believed that a great secret once existed in Machu Picchu. A secret so explosive that its very traces were buried, left forgotten in the sands of time. However, legends of this magnitude seldom die. And so the rumors began. Lots of them. Yet they all carried a single message at the core.

The world would come to a standstill and eventually end. But there was a single object that could prevent this great catastrophe from occurring. And it would bear the sigil and face of their great God Viracocha.

Keeping this very thought in mind, the United Kingdom sent a team of its twenty best archaeologists to the site of Machu Picchu on the Andes. Acclaimed as the hardest exploration ever undertaken, the British were now trudging through time, money, and public hope in the quest to find something of value.

All this planning at the insistence of one woman.

Juliana Herbert was twenty-five. Her description of herself would be that she is of average height, slim, and has a passive nature for an adventurous heart underneath. She thought she looked rather unattractive, but a short chat with her male colleagues would reveal otherwise.

A fiercely independent woman, her childhood love for history made her take a course in Mythology and finally use that qualification to enter the British Special Services in Archaeology. If you asked her about her one true love, she would probably reply with the Incans and the Andes mountains.

Thus, it was but natural that she would head this expedition, a person with such a plethora of both interest and knowledge in the history of the Incan civilization. However, as she was soon to find out, even learned minds occasionally get their minds blown, and their beliefs surprised straight.

ᔛ✦ᔢ

The god Viracocha, according to Incan sagas, was the great creator deity of the world. He created everything, from the celestial bodies to the oceans and tides that obey their tidings. He created the humans and let them roam the earth. It is believed that Viracocha did all this and then walked into the Pacific Ocean and never came back. However, he would reappear in times of immense crisis and show the humans the way out of misery and into prosperity.

But there were others.

A few believed that Viracocha was not a mystical God but rather a humble human. A human who rose to God-like stature because of his deeds. Arguments arise over the deity being worshipped by the Mayans as Quetzalcoatl, the feathered serpent God, and it was never the Incans in the first place.

It was these questions that Julianna hoped to answer, or at least find some clues to, as the helicopter touched down in Cuzco. A posse of black cats swarmed over her, assisting her easy passage into the waiting car outside. As she walked toward it, a feeling of excitement swept over her. She felt like her life's greatest dream was coming true. Anxiety negated carefulness and her absent-minded nature failed to notice a shady figure standing discreetly behind a lamppost; her head bowed low. Although you couldn't be sure from a distance, it looked like he was smiling broadly or frowning, depending on his facial tics. And within a second, he vanished.

Julianna, still preoccupied with her thoughts, revved the engine, and sped off.

₨✦⇒

Under the examining room, Sunil had an underground lab for super urgent assignments. Cut off from the rest of the RAW building, this vast expanse of scientific marvels had helped solve innumerable cases. And today, they were using it one more time.

Trix had assembled the entire team for this one. They were a seven-strong team. Sunil, Trix, Madhav, Raghav, Sahil, Divyesh, and the new entry, Hafeez.

Madhav Agarwal. A techno-legend, he lived, breathed, and slept technology. A true master of the Digital Age, there was no gizmo beyond his reach and no tech concept beyond his understanding. He is a graduate of IIT Kharagpur, and his rank is 6th best in the whole nation. He was RAW intelligence's backbone and one of the so-called Saptrishis. He had worked for Infosys before joining RAW for four times the pay of his old firm. Here at RAW, all his needs and desires were fulfilled.

Raghav Badar. India's leading psychologist. He had the ability to predict thoughts, emotions, and even future courses of action with effortless ease. His predictive success rate came up to a staggering 96 %, one of the highest in the world. RAW acquired him for their need of the hour back in 2003. His impeccable skills had him ink a permanent deal with them.

Sahil Raj. I am an ardent science fan and a full-time particle physicist. Honorary doctorate from the Indian Institute of Science and a recipient of the CV Raman Award for Scientific Cognizance. At 30, Sahil exuded a kind of quaint aura that belied his curious personality. Smart and intuitive, it seemed the keys to the wonders of science were in his back pocket.

Divyesh Malhotra. A perfect example of the ideal soldier. He was a leader of the Paratroopers regiment and a supremely skilled agent, trained in five different martial arts and spoke six languages. He was RAW's personal James Bond. He even complimented his nickname in attire. Known to be fierce to foes and gentle to friends, he was a great asset to have when 'in the zone.'

And finally, Hafeez Shah. A boy at 22, quite new, unfamiliar to everyone, yet unfazed by the inattention. He entered RAW on an internship, but his fanciful exploits and quick thinking in previous missions got him reassigned to intelligence. Hafeez, however, had talent. He was a builder. Whatever tech Madhav needed, Hafeez could make. He was an integral part of the missions, often with his inventions coming in really handy.

This was the team.

'Guys, we have a situation here,' he started.

'Our contact in Africa has just been found dead. He was last seen with a woman of about 25 years, blonde, of North American descent. And this fax that we have here, he said, holding up the paper. 'We don't know where it came from. It is a serious issue, for this means that our contact's identity was leaked.'

'Madhav, 48 hours. That's all. Can you get me visuals on the murder? His ERC transponder must be working. Can you check?' Sunil was indeed dumbfounded. He knew that if the killers could send a fax, then they would have surely found the transponder. But it was worth a try.

Suddenly, a thought came to him.

'Divyesh? Can you make a call to the Defense Ministry? Tell them that it's urgent and needs immediate attention.

'Okay Sunil will do,' said Divyesh. As he turned, he felt a hand on his shoulder. Sunil.

'Divyesh, when they ask you for a reason, just tell them that the moon showed a little less of himself yesterday.'

'Huh?' thought Divyesh. That was a random sentence to say. But when it came to Sunil, you couldn't really know much. He smiled and walked out the door.

CHAPTER 2

The cold bit him hard. He was shivering, and yet he plowed on. He needed to reach HQ before the recognized time was over. Being late was not an option. The package, a small, silvery-gray ball with a milky substance, was the reason for this whole avalanche of trouble.

He knew the job was hard, but it was worth the money. Every bit of it. He knew the rules. He knew the stakes. He also knew he couldn't afford slip-ups. The Russians had given him enough education on that particular subject. Especially on deals like this. Seventy billion dollars for a single sphere? The fuck?

The messenger continued to trudge on, until he arrived at an ornately carved palace, seeming to appear out of the blue. Its black décor stood out in stark contrast to the white snow all around it. He was running now, and he finally reached the iron gates that stood sentinel to the hallowed portals of this underground dungeon fortress.

The intercom was on the gate. There was no security. They didn't need it. Less than sixty people know of the castle's existence. He pressed the button, and the intercom buzzed to life.

A deep crackling sound, and then a familiar voice.

"Da?"

"I have the package. Request confirmation for entry."

"Come in."

ॐ ✦ ॐ

Julianna emerged from her hotel lobby, famished. She checked her watch. 2:30 A.M. The car should have been here already. Seeing no sign of the car, she stood by the lamppost, admiring Peru in all its scintillating morning stillness. The street was completely deserted, apart from a few lights flickering above as if giving company. Being a cautious woman, she quickly scanned the streets for signs of suspicion. None at first sight. She looked and looked and looked and….

There! In the bushes behind the garbage dump, a lone human's silhouette stood out, crouching in the shadows. Although he was hidden, his face was clear to Julianna.

That face, she would never forget.

It seemed to hover, forming different facades of green and red over a face that was barely human.

Immediately, her feet were on the move, trying to get closer. But the figure did something impossible. He turned around and, from his crouch, sprung up like a dog and scaled the massive six-foot wall in mere seconds. However, Julianna wasn't shocked by the maneuver. The 'thing' had left something behind. She quickly ran over and picked up the fallen item. It was a necklace of sorts. Its apex paraded a symbol that flummoxed Julianna as soon as she saw it.

A K.

An ornately fashioned K, with some intricate design. It seemed to be made of wood and had something written behind it in an unknown tongue:

23!@!#!##!2434

"What in the world?" she thought.

Her car had still not arrived.

ಙ◆ಐ

Meanwhile, in RAW's underground bunker lab, Madhav had decoded the ERC transponder and was now playing its last moments to the team on the projector.

'Okay. So the guy must have been walking through the jungle when we heard the jungle go quiet. And now, suddenly, there is a flash, and a hypodermic bullet is shot into his chest, Sunil concluded.

'This means that they were prepared and knew he was coming. Then, our contacts must have been compromised. We must inform defense,' said Divyesh, in typical military strategy.

Hafeez, who was quiet all this time, perked up suddenly.

'Uh, Madhav? Could you replay the video?' he asked.

'Yeah, sure, no problem.'

'Move it to screen two, where he gets shot by the bullet. Yeah, just a bit more…. a little more… there! Stop right there.' Hafeez jumped.

Everyone was now fully invested in where Hafeez was planning to take this.

'Okay, everyone, I want you to think about this. The moment the bullet was shot, it hit the transponder. This means that our contact didn't die or get paralyzed. They must have aimed at the transponder.'

'How could they possibly know?' asked Divyesh.

' Guys, watch closely. Where I stopped the video, zoom into the toggle, and see the top right-hand side, Hafeez said.

'Do you guys see what I'm seeing? The significance of it?'

Sunil was shocked. An unexpected, unforeseen development.

'What the hell!' he thought to himself, as he began to think about what he had just seen.

ఙ ✦ ౚ

Africa was called the Wild Jewel for a reason. It was the most densely populated forest area until the colonial period when colonizers salvaged the resources from the continent. Centuries of exploitation had led to Africa's primitive stereotype when it came to development.

So, it seemed quite contradictory that an ultra-modern technological hub existed at its heart. Its entrance was hidden by dense foliage, and on top was a small, unassuming cottage. On entering, there existed a secret button to transmogrify the hut into the entrance.

Sitting inside its rooms, staring at the LED TVs on the wall depicting CCTV footage from major countries in the world, a man smiled. He layered his legs over the seams of the table as he watched the proceedings. Satisfaction crept up.

The man they called the Burning Flame stood up from his desk to peer out at the vast warehouse that served as an assembly line for his futuristic machine toys, many of whose technologies hadn't yet been discovered by western minds. Kino-technic guns, tanker-bankers, residual revolvers, you name it, he had it.

The man imagined the strategy he had laid out three months ago. All was according to plan. If everything went well, Africa would rise again. Rise from the ashes like a phoenix to regain its place among the best.

But for that, he had work to do. There were wars to be fought and machines to be made.

Slowly turning, he returned to staring at the TVs.

A new acquisition had been the Belgian typo that had failed. Failure was not accepted. Failure was outlawed. Success determined the fate of his country.

Africa would be great again. And he would be at his helm.

CHAPTER 3

The man trembled as the ornately covered brass doors of the castle slowly opened and gave way into the hall. The man scurried in, the package seeming heavier with each passing step. As he walked, he gazed up at the huge portraits the wall was adorned with. The portraits depicted generations of a family, the family that the world feared most.

The Lorenzos.

Been in the crime world for generations, mastered the art of deceptive living, and now King of their own army, a Lorenzo seal of protection could get you anything you needed, and anywhere you wanted.

Each generation of the Lorenzos stared down at the messenger as though assuaging the contents of the packet. The packet grew even more heavier.

The hall finally ended at a double-locked steel door. As he approached, he neither knocked on the door nor tried to pry it open. The instructions had been clear.

'Don't touch the doors. The doors open themselves.'

He felt his breath harden as he stood right in front of the door. His heart raced, questioning what, just what was inside that needed so much security.

1….2….3….4…5. he heard a switch. Slowly, the gears turned. He felt the locks being unlocked. With a loud creak, the door opened.

The messenger walked into the highly lit hall, making sense of the décor inside. It was a castle lair, completely done up in black marble. He looked up to see a stairway leading up to a throne. On the throne, two wolves gushed out as armrests. He gazed at the person sitting on the throne. His complete body was hidden by a long black coat, except for his face. His eyes, those eyes, were a mystical gray. One look, and you knew he was evil. He controlled the entire Russian Mafia, he was the overlord of the underworld, and he was the King of hell. And yet, his face had a certain childishness. One you could trust. Something that made him the favorite for political and celebrity secrets.

This was Daniel Lorenzo. 23rd descendant and scion of the Lorenzo clan.

Daniel slowly lifted his face up to look at the messenger. The package was soon his object of focus. He tilted his head to one side as if examining the messenger with childish curiosity.

'Give it to me,' a raspy, slithering voice hissed.

ॐ ✦ ॐ

Julianna now sat in her comfortable tent outside the base excavation site of Machu Picchu. It had been an hour-long journey to get there, which was made possible by the Peruvian railways.

They were on the train that bore the namesake of the explorer who first stepped on the treasure of Machu Picchu. Hiram Bingham.

An explorer with the eye for the unconventional, Hiram was credited with revealing the secrets of the massive Inca empire that existed on the Andes mountains. Soon, Machu Picchu became the face and symbol of Peru.

However, Julianna was still intrigued by the K that lay in her hands. The inscriptions on the back continued to baffle her, even though she had double-checked with every possible existing language in the world, from Macedonian Greek to Latin and even India's regional dialects. No matches. She put it away, closing the drawers for another day. There would always be time to check again.

She now waited for news of the first expedition she sent out. Her hopes were really high as she was certain there were some signs that Viracocha was there.

With a soft press of the zip, the tent opened to her two lieutenants, John, and Stacy.

'Julianna?' they called.

'Yeah, I'm here. Report on findings?'

'We got something. A marker, I suppose, of Viracocha, but it is in a language that we couldn't understand. We want to examine it closely, though,' they declared.

'Okay, I'll see to it.' Julianna was thoroughly excited.

As they moved out, John stopped.

'Julianna? One more thing, he said.

'Yeah?'

'There is something written on it. In Russian, of all things.'

'What do you mean, Russian?' Julianna looked bewildered.

"Our Russian personnel translated it to 'The God arrives when the dog survives.' We have no clue what it means, though."

Julianna thought for a second and made up her mind.

'Let's go,' she said.

This was another problem. Another mystery for her crew. Julianna felt that doubt slowly creep into her, thinking this might not have been as easy as he thought it would be.

And this time, she wasn't going to be disappointed.

ℰ✦ℭ

In Africa, the 'Burning Flame' turned his eyes to the package at his feet. This package had mysteriously appeared at the foot of the cottage the previous night, bearing a message.

'Greetings from the Lorenzos. We realize the failure with the Belgians has led you to believe your machines are powerless. However, we have acquired the necessary materials to jumpstart your machines into full-scale use. All we require is unending support and technology for the machines. A bundle of the amount we requested is sitting as collateral in case of failure to uphold our promise. And remember, no slip-ups from either side.'

It was signed by Daniel Lorenzo. At the front of the package was the seal that both terrified and graced people for centuries. The Lorenzo insignia.

But what was truly scary was the huge covering of cotton and thermocouple inside the package. It was unwrapped. The object that came out brought forth guffawing and approval.

'Exactly what I needed, my friend,' the man said to himself.

'Take it inside.'

It was time for the final trial.

◦✦◦

Sunil squinted as they observed the face that had now appeared in the top right corner.

'Looks African American to me,' Raghav concluded, much to the approval of the assembled.

'Let's put this into the database feed to crosscheck with the World Criminal List and the regional Indian list as well,' Sunil said. Right then, his phone rang. It was the Defense Minister.

A call he couldn't refuse.

After three long breaths, he picked up the call.

'Hello? This is Sunil.'

'Sunil, what is this update that everyone is on about? And how far along the trail are we? Why do you want to activate the express network? As far as I've been informed, an agent's death does not warrant the need to use the express network,' the Minister said.

'You are right, Sir, but the problem is that he is dead in a very mysterious and untimely situation. Also, we received a fax from his killers with a close-up photo of his dead body, indicating our cover was blown. And yes, I said killers,' Sunil countered.

After that, there was silence as the Minister calculated the grim possibilities.

'Hmm. Okay, I will make the call to activate the network. But mind you, no mistakes. I want a complete and clean retrieval of information. Africa, right? I'll phone the authorities. Oh, and in what country did the incident happen?' he asked.

'Sir, about that…. we don't really know. The transponder was taken only after entry into forested areas. Hard to gauge the country by the forest type,

Sir; they look very identical to most vegetation,' Sunil replied.

"In that case, find out the country first. If this is really a blown-up case, we need to take care of it. RAW is the finest we have. Sunil, you have my permission to employ any method to solve this case. Get this bloody problem out of RAW's hands," the Minister said with a tone of finality.

Yes, Sir, will do. Thank you so much,' said Sunil.

'Sir, are the protocols I sent over approved?'

He only got a click in response.

Sunil put the phone back, sighed, and went back to the team.

'Guys, I have news. The Minister of Defense wants us to employ any methods to solve this case. But first, he asked to find the country of our agent's death so as to speak with their authorities. That is a task in itself. So, I propose we begin an operation. An operation to retrieve our agent's body and also find out the cause, consequence and effect of death. Alright?'

Sunil decided this was the best way to take forward the case since an all-out attack might not be favored by higher officials.

'Madhav? Any luck with the face yet?' he asked.

'Nada. Still working on it, though. Indian databases have no matches. We will have to thoroughly check international records. It might take at least four days, he concluded. Madhav looked at Sunil with hopeful eyes.

"Alright, take your time. This is important to the case," said Sunil.

Hafeez suddenly opened up.

'Guys. Shouldn't our operation have a name? Like, for official purposes?' he asked, being practical.

'He's right,' Sunil said. 'Any ideas for a name?'

'I have an idea,' said Divyesh. 'Let's call it Operation Sooraj since our best chances of solving it are in daylight.'

Sunil nodded. Everyone consented.

'Okay then! Operation Sooraj, it is!'

CHAPTER 4

Cuzco is the capital of Peru. It is the cultural, technological, and economic hub of the country. Therefore, it isn't a surprise that Cuzco has its own representations and memorabilia of the Incan Empire.

One of the best is Saqsaywaman.

Saqsaywaman existed merely as a subculture of Machu Picchu before its individual attention gathered cultural interest. This was a separate Incan city, complete with its own décor and extravaganza.

The biggest mystery about Saqsaywaman existed not inside it but rather on its wall. Huge chunks of stone, seemingly of highly varied shapes and sizes, all magically put together to form an imposing stone wall along the perimeter of the city, all done before the advent of alloys or even any form of modern civil engineering. Millennia, ahead of their time, the Incans were terrific builders, as is seen by their imposing stone structures. Rituals and worship formed an important part of every Incan's life.

Today was Inti Raymi. Across the Andes, from the tip of Argentina to the reaches of Colombia, indigenous Incans gathered for the southern hemisphere's winter solstice to honor the ancient Sun God Inti. It was the 24th of June.

The thing was bent low in a room at the ruins well after closing time. His cloak had been thrown off, revealing his true body and shape, away from magical concealment. He was in the sunroom, where all sacrifices to Inti were made.

'San………Jama………Waseya,' he chanted.

With each word, he threw a piece of a plant into a burning fire at the altar. He continued chanting till the climax. And then…. He felt his inner self awaken. Become stronger again. He was rejuvenated and renewed.

Powers were replenished, and he put his cloak back on, ready to report to the council.

ജ✦ര

Juliannna trudged on, completely unfazed by the cold around her, courtesy of high altitudes. Her focus was completely on the marker.

The car took tantalisingly slow turns due to the intense amount of hairpin bends that one needed to traverse before the city arrived. Finally, they were at the entrance.

A pair of military officers stood guard as their major stepped up and checked for identification.

'Julianna Herbert? Of British Archaeology?' the major asked, eyebrows rising higher with each question.

'Yes, precisely. Now, are we allowed in or not?' Julianna asked with a tinge of haughtiness.

'Of course. Enjoy your visit.'

I'm sure I will.

And with this entrée, she marched off into the site.

'Alright now, John, tell me where it is,' she asked.

John pointed a finger toward a site marked "No Entry." Funny how "Now Entry" usually means complete access when you are a government official. Sighing, she opened the flap and tucked it under the cordoning tape. As she made her way through the muck that was in the excavation, she found the hole where the object was first found. Her heart is leaping; she eagerly puts her hands into it to find……. Nothing, it wasn't there?!!

'John, Stacy, where is it?' Julianna asked, anger consuming her completely. Her assistants turned toward her.

'I don't know…. Don't know Julianna. Somebody must have taken it when we left, both answered in unison.

'What? So you were the only ones here?' Julianna was finished, and everything she had worked for would be gone if that object hadn't been found.

Who took the marker? The looming question in her legs suddenly gave way, and her world went blank.

₧ ✦ ₨

Nearly 15 hours had passed since the messenger's departure, and still, Daniel hadn't touched the package. There was something holding him back. Something is constantly reminding him of its spectacular power. He managed nothing but a weak nod when questioned by his aides as to why his package hadn't been touched.

Finally, coming out of his trance, he got up from his throne and stepped down with soft, gliding steps. His long coat swept the floor like a coiled snake waiting to strike.

But for Daniel. As he walked toward the pedestal where it was kept, he thought about the weight of the mission. The entire organization was at risk. He did not think he could not do the job, but that doubt always creeps in from places unknown. He also had his family's name to live up to. He felt completely like Coleridge's Mariner, surrounded by fickle-minded people who never seemed to be faithful to a side. By doing so, Daniel displayed a rare show of emotion, almost unheard of from the underworld don.

'Enough is enough,' he thought. And he opened the package, hands trembling in the excitement of being the person to lay his hands upon this super strong power. The package opened, and the sphere was revealed to him as he cradled it in his hands.

Daniel held the sphere gingerly, as he would a newborn. As he peered into it, a swirling mass of milky white zoomed around the sphere, and he saw his own eyes, those very ones, stare back unquestioningly at him.

The thought of such power parting with him was impossible to believe. And yet, his friend in Africa needed it. So he would do it.

It wasn't all for friendship, though. Sometimes, it's better to hide than to hunt.

കൗ ✦ ര

They say if you don't like critics, don't do anything new or interesting. But what if there were no critics?

Burning Flame was a live example. Any failure was made sure to be concealed. Even then, if news leaked and if critics were found, they were…exterminated. No trouble, no questions asked.

Dictatorships formed the basis of the Burning Flame's desire to be the best in the world. Complete unending devotion to the leader. Over the years, he had grown from a small suburban boy in the streets of Nigeria to the head of an internationally feared and reputed weapons depot. His inventions were light years ahead of their time, although it was really hard to believe that a boy with no real formal education could formulate or even dream of such gizmos. But he was different.

With his genius, shrewdness, and, of course, the support he received from the Somalis, he could ensure his meteoric rise. The amazing toys that the Somali boys stole offshore had helped him gain a strong foothold in weapons making.

As a matter of fact, Somalia was precisely where he was headed right now. A meeting was in order with an extremist chief, Saud Batashyayi. Maybe he would get a few new spoils to explore and understand.

All this after a rocky, 200-mile stretch of pure desert terrain navigated with a rusty old Land Cruiser. Ire Oku, as he was known in his native tongue of Igbo, sat back onto the railings of the car, sighing.

Sometimes, life makes you pay really hard for success. Real hard.

ဆော ✦ ဘ

Voices. Then silence. Drops sounded distant, water trickling onto her face. Julianna suddenly came to consciousness. She woke up bruised, tired, and dazed. She looked around. It was pitch dark, except for some sort of light source some distance away.

As her eyes adjusted to the darkness around her, she noticed a few things simultaneously. She was in a kind of tunnel, with strange markings of some primitive Incan form on the wall. Her memory regained presence, and she remembered falling through a hole. But then, the top of the tunnel should have broken in, shouldn't it? Then why was it so solid?

Her gaze fell on the floor where there was a single sign described on the stones. An arrow, pointing straight ahead.

Julianna felt this loneliness and helplessness that was doing absolutely nothing to ease her mind about the situation she found herself in. Suddenly, she saw the light source flicker a little in the dark, just for a split second. So, she did the most logical thing. She got up and ran.

She soon caught up with the first light source, a flaming torch. The sight of it provided some form of relief to her. Julianna unhooked it from the wall and walked until she found a set of stairs. A few steps, and then the stairway was blocked by a huge stone door. Markings of the ancient Incan language Quipu were strung across the surface. There was a keyhole at the very corner of the door, almost invisible to an inobservant eye. However, Julianna was anything but inobservant. She examined the key slot. It was in the shape of a K.

'A k?' she thought.

And then she remembered the locket.

৯০✦୧৩

Divyesh pulled up his rucksack and made his way over to the very crowded Delhi metro station. He had just been through that ridiculously amazing session at RAW, and now it was time to head back and relax.

Divyesh, although technically a full RAW employee, still worked undercover for the Defense Ministry. Divyesh had some say in all decisions regarding RAW. Even the decision to allow any eliminative strategy had been proposed to him. Operation Sooraj had, essentially, been his.

He got off at the home stop and made his way across to the RAW Apartments, which were the most highly guarded regions in the city, on par with the ISRO residences. Residents were required to undergo eye scans, fingerprint scans and even a full genetic checkup with a Gene-IE before being allowed complete access. He walked up to his apartment, where his old friend, Chand, was standing guard.

'Chand bhai, kaise ho? Kya haal chaal?' he asked, exchanging pleasantries for recognition reasons.

'Hum, theek hai bhai. Aap toh chaliye, check karne ki koi zaroorat nahi hai,' Chand replied, in the tone of people who immediately fall under the spell of a quick, sweet conversation.

Security checks were done, and he walked over to the lift that took him to the 9th floor. Divyesh lived in 909. In his opinion, it is the fanciest number on the entire block.

Divyesh conducted his usual routine check of looking for the piece of red strap he had placed under the door. It was still there. Perfect. He locked his phone and then unlocked the door.

There, lying on the sofa, was a package. Divyesh was immediately on high alert, taking quick searches everywhere. Finding no one, he wondered about the effectiveness of his checking mechanism.

He went toward the package. It was from the Defense Ministry. There was a note.

'Divyesh, the Inter-Governmental conference on Weapons is being held in Copenhagen from the 5th of August to the 8th. You're going. Be ready.'

The note was signed by the Minister.

Divyesh checked his calendar. The 5th was the day after tomorrow. Ah, the peril of RAWagain. It was going to be a very long night.

Sadly, he was right.

CHAPTER 5

'Sit,' he ordered. Troboyan Lazvensky obeyed. Once the head of the informatics division at the General Secretary's Office, a grave inquiry into the deaths of one of Russia's foremost singers, unfortunately, exposed his impressive array of illegal hedge funds that were used to hoard money to an undisclosed or rather, undiscovered location. It's funny how life messes with you when you've done nothing, and life does nothing when you've messed up everything.

And now, because of karma, or fate, or luck, or just really bad timing, he was here, at the Labraska, the winter palace of the Russian Mafia. It was unfathomable that the government would take the aid of the Mafia to break a suspect. But nobody argues with the Mafia's reputation and the results they could produce.

'Tie this to your eyes,' the masked man said. Lazvensky was not answering. He wanted to remain as silent as possible, wait for these people to lose patience and do something rash. There was a huge circle around him, all armed men. All with AK-47s. Old school. Jack and Jill. Back to kill.

'Tie this now!' he barked. Troboyan didn't have a choice. He obliged, soon severing his eye's connection to the proceedings.

Blam!

A whack across his cheek, followed by one on his stomach and the final cracker on his ribs. Pain rose faster than the bile.

'What ….do. You…. want?' Troboyan finally managed.

'We want your answer. Tell us where you sent the money. Tell us now, or mind you, there are things worse than death, the man replied, a flash of machoism for that dialogue. Well appreciated by his mind for that remark, the masked man loaded his gun and placed it on the victim's ears. No sound from Troboyan.

'Last chance, tell us what we want. Battered and bruised as you are, a little truth won't hurt. Come on, spill.'

'No. You will…. Never… get…. anything…. From…. Me. My …. Dying. promise…. I will…. Always win.'

Troboyan was now completely off the hook, and his mind was shutting itself off, completely compartmentalizing itself, saving energy and precious memory space.

There was only one thing that could be done now.

Crack!

The masked one snuffed the gun and put it back in its holster. Another mission was completed. He ordered his men to pick up the body and make it bio-degradable. While doing so, he found a note had come undone from one of Troboyan's pockets.

He picked it up, read its contents, and a wide smile inched up across his face.

'Well, well, well,' he said.

Wasn't Daniel going to be happy? He folded the paper, shot the already cold body a couple of times, and went back, not turning once.

Old school. Jack and Jill. Back to kill.

ꕥ✦ꕥ

Somalia was a very, very difficult place to acclimatize to, as he was so well aware of it. They had arrived at Mogadishu, the capital of this hunger-stricken country. One of the most impoverished nations of the world, Somalia was in danger of a quick wipeout of most of its people. Hence, people find it hard to find happiness in most things when their attention is mostly focused on trying to live. It was in this scenario that the Burning Flame found himself. But he had a connection. He was African, and so were they. Two descendants of the same ancestors. Propagators of the greatness of the Cradle of Life. Africa made great again.

His goal quickly shifted to thinking about the economic possibilities of Somalia. The country was impoverished, malnourished, underprivileged and, most of the time, unaccounted for.

Piracy offered a way out of that. A chance to solve a crisis, join the missing dots. An option to lift upward from the slums to rejoin the greats. The only problem? It wasn't really legal.

That was his proposition. A little legal help in exchange for the new acquisition from smugglers.

'Quite a sight, sir?' one of his comrades asked.

'Sadat, I'd shut up if I were you,' replied Burning Flame in a sweet, I'll-kill-you tone.

The car lurched to a stop in front of a dilapidated building. There was nothing particularly suspicious about the building except that the outside was untidy as hell, and yet the entrance had a sterilized retina scanner for the door. If anybody chanced upon the building, curiosity was sure to be aroused.

Burning Flame got out, surveyed the scene, and slowly rambled to the entrance. 'This better be a hell of a good thing,' he thought.

Oh, the irony.

The K surely increased Julianna's prospect of a new find. Breathless, she pressed the locket to the space. It fit. As it slowly went in, Julianna felt her heart pounding. The start of something new. Something exciting.

The locket had fit itself in. She waited…. and nothing happened. It was then that she noticed an arrow mark pointing upwards. She did the natural thing. She pushed the locket up.

With a loud crash, the rocks started to move. The sound was deafening as rocks crackled and moved to make way in the middle for a beautifully hidden rock to be revealed. This rock was engraved. Engraved. It was also inlaid with what looked like jade and… lapis lazuli. The divine jewels of the superior beings.

She bent down to survey her handiwork. A soft dusting of the rock revealed…lettering? The stone was engraved in the ENGLISH ALPHABET?! It looked like it was written in a poetic format, with words lined on the surface of the stone. She stepped closer to the stone for a closer inspection.

She found parts of the rock had been cut out and chipped away. The rest of the poem, however, is a treasure trove.

"The world will rise and fall again,

For life or death, you must bargain,

____ will be the guide to thee

To save the world and live in harmony.

Viracocha's secret you must uncover,

The lost city must be discovered.

It is in Villa.

To reignite the lost Sapa Inca."

There were some missing pieces in the puzzle, but Julianna was confident that her team could crack through it. She was just about to pick it up when a thought struck her.

How was she going to get out?

ℙ✦ℛ

The suitcase felt heavy as he hauled it up the gangway plank. A pretty air hostess smiled, welcomed, and winked at Divyesh. He got that a lot. Anyways, his seat was taken 23B. He moved over, seeing his seat was empty, placed his baggage in the overhead compartment and sat down.

He was just going through the magazine cover when a gruff voice said,'Excuse me?'

Surprised at the tone of his words, he turned to see… a man. A really tiny one at that. About 4 feet 9 inches, at most. Ulcers covered his skin, and his face was pockmarked, probably from a childhood defect. It was his voice that was so disrespectful.

'Move out! I need to go in,' he said again, not very sure what words to put after that. Divyesh, thinking queerly about his sanity, let him through.

The man came in, put his baggage down and sat, settling comfortably in. Buckling his seatbelt, he looked out of the window and then at Divyesh.

'What a wonderful start to the day?' he exclaimed at Divyesh.

Flash!

A jolt of electricity hit Divyesh. That voice! He had heard it somewhere. Somewhere before. But where?

He was sure he had never seen the guy. But he realized the texture and roughness of his voice were very eventful things because he remembered it.

Divyesh didn't respond, just nodded. The man turned his neck back to the window and went back to admiring the view. Something about him seemed so mechanical, so eerie, so machine-like. But he put that down to the man's nature. Ex-military, maybe?

He was just about to voice his thoughts when the overhead intercom crackled.

'Good afternoon, ladies, and gentlemen. You are now sitting inside a time bomb. Enjoy.'

Chapter 6

The cave is...... boring. It doesn't stand out as impressive or as a marvel of the work of nature. Its geographical location also doesn't strike any bells.

But there it was, on the edges of Vietnam's biggest city, Ho Chi Minh. Named after the president of Vietnam's Democratic Republic and the progenitor of modern Vietnam, Ho Chi Minh was laid out with a mission. A mission to revamp and alter the face of Cochin China.

But there is something better than that. Something that is more famous than the city itself. The Ho Chi Minh Trail.

The story of the Ho Chi Minh Trail is a way to understand the war the Vietnamese fought with the Americans. It symbolizes how the Vietnamese used their limited resources to great advantage.

This trail was an immense network of roads and footpaths which was used to transport men and materials from the north to the south of Vietnam. This trail was quick and efficient, equipped with support bases which enabled the Vietnamese to oust the Americans. It was a powerful symbol.

On this trail, in the outskirts, stood a dilapidated building. Roof aging, wall paint peeling off and floorboards dusty. In short, a ghost house.

But this was the cave.

No, the cave was never overground. It is always underground. A swiveling bookshelf reveals a steep set of stairs leading down to…. Inwasmet.

The holy council of Incas.

And he was on the stand today. Today, he would reveal the truth to the council. What truth?

That the secret was not confined to them. That they weren't orphaned. The British woman had come so close to the truth. There was no guarantee she wouldn't have found it. He thought of the council. The scroll. The British lady had come with a mission. To sow the seed of knowledge. His job was to uproot it.

Filled with renewed purpose, he hurried down the firelit passage in anticipation of the results of his stand. He could hear the drums beating.

His heart followed.

The masked one, the one called Preziyan, walked slowly toward the gilded doors of the Labraska's main office room. Daniel's. In his hand was the note.

After he shot the body, this note was discovered. What does it say? It had four co-ordinates marked on it, probably the various addresses where his money was holed up. But they would never know if this was a trap, and the note was kept there to purposely catch it.

Swiveling thoughts pushed away, he slid the doors and walked into the office, where Daniel was on a phone call.

'Uh……. Yeah. I'll send the amount shortly. You wouldn't want the Chekha on you, right? Send me the body and the parcel, and the due payment is yours. Or else…. remember. No mistakes.'

As Daniel put down the phone, he had already created the seed of doubt in Preziyan's mind. A thousand questions were looming in his mind.

'Da?'

'Yes, boss. We found something. A note. It had four co-ordinates on it. Probably could be the resting place of the bounty. This could also be a trap whose threats we can neutralize. In short, the situation is under control. For now, Preziyan said, assuaging Daniel's firm belief in him.

'Should we check these co-ordinates, senor?'

'Ok. Bring me the results soon.

'Si senor.'

Wait, what? Spanish. But the truth was a bit different. Preziyan may have been masked, but his story is a legend. And yes, he was an ex-captain of the Spanish Armada. And, truly, the Crusades just seemed to start. And the last time it happened; things got shit bad. It was about to get worse.

ॐ ✦ ૱

The lights came on to show something that the Burning Flame hadn't expected.

A suit.

A freaking three-piece suit.

His lead blew off the top.

'What the actual fuck? What do you mean by presenting me with a bloody suit?' he barked.

The chief of the pirates sat directly beside him. All of 31, Saud Batashyayi was a formidable man. His all-powerful army wasn't the crux of his fearful personality.

He was 5 foot 4, heavily built, had a barrel-like chest, 22-inch biceps, and some serious macho buff. Some type of intimidation. Normally, it was either brains or brawns. This man was a unique combination of both, which enabled him to access some high contacts, get clout and also command the biggest number of Somalian pirates. Ever.

Definitely not a man to be trifled with. But he was talking to the Burning Flame. The pride of the pride.

'Sir. Not true. This is no ordinary suit. This incredibly high-tech goody bag has a ton of surprises. You like, you take. A one-time offer. Because this useful to us also.'

Burning Flame thought about the authenticity of the suit. Hand-made, judging from the cut. Textiles from the Balkans, looking at the richness of the texture. It was highly probable that this piece was from a weapon depot.

'Okay. Show me.'

ೞ ✦ ೞ

Julianna was done for. She had come down to this godforsaken place for a sign of Viracocha. Instead, it seemed like now, she was the sign that people needed to find.

She heard the sound of drilling far away, up above, quite some time before they reached her. Might as well rest for a while. Surprisingly, the air didn't seem stale. It was almost…. Fresh?

She surveyed the stone again. There's not much to help her out of here. She didn't have to personally take out the stone, as the lines were now committed to memory. The lapis lazuli glinted in the wake of her torch. There were no lit passages here.

'Seems like there is no way out of here,' she sighed to herself. Dejected, she walked over to one of the broken rocks and sat down. She was surely tired. And very famished. What she needed was food and rest. Both of which were near impossibilities down here.

As her thoughts wandered, her leg moved slightly, brushing against a particular rock. Something rough. Julianna bent down and took the piece into her hands.

There was a lot of soot covering the rock. Julianna opened up her rucksack and cleaned up the rock. As she cleaned it, she noticed it started glinting. She applied a little more polishing until… there it was.

A fist-sized rock of lapis lazuli. Inlaid with gold.

She couldn't believe her eyes. She quickly set to work, cleaning each stone. Each cleansing revealed more and more gold.

It was then that it hit her.

The signs, the lighting, everything. She felt slightly overwhelmed as she realized her whereabouts.

This was no ordinary cave she had fallen into. It was a vault.

The vault of Manco Inca.

Chapter 7

Divyesh was now on complete alert. Meanwhile, the intercom still continued.

'This time, we will succeed. Fifteen times has our brotherhood been thwarted. Not anymore! For years, the stronghold of imperialism has been silent. Not anymore!'

Now, Divyesh was in a highly calculated state. What if this guy was a lunatic fighting against imperialism?

"You think I'm a lunatic? Fine. Do you know why? Because history doesn't treat everyone fairly. You succeed; you are a genius, a rebel. But fail, and you are a megalomaniac. An outcast, a lunatic. So I'm the fool here? Do you think this will fail? We'll see," said the voice on the intercom, as if reading his thoughts.

Divyesh gathered his courage.

'Who are you? What do you want?' he shouted above the din. It was heard in the control room of the flight, the cockpit.

'Good question, my friend. Who am I? I am the future. What do I want? I want a person. Just one. And

I know he's on this flight. Divyesh Malhotra. Come to me.'

All this time, Divyesh was intrigued, and the mechanical man turned to face him. He reached into the side pocket of the jeans he wore. He then took out a syringe. It was filled with a golden-colored substance, milky in composition.

Suddenly, Divyesh turned, and instincts told him threats were around. He looked at the man, then at the syringe, and knew it was going to be a long journey to Copenhagen if he made it out alive.

Since Divyesh was of a field agent's build, a simple swing of the shoulder brought in a crunching shit to the man's arm, releasing the syringe. Next, Divyesh adopted an Indian staple, giving four quick slaps before instantly hitting pressure points, ending with the solar plexus. That man was now officially paralyzed.

Oh yes, you get the point. The whole mess, chaos, confusion, and general mayhem. After a few satellite phone calls, he realized something: that the flight had gone really quiet. Everybody was looking at something beyond him. To the cockpit. He turned.

The man was completely covered. Completely. Not one part was exposed. He held the gun in one hand and the syringe in another.

'Now, now, easy there. No need to fight; let's resolve this easily,' said Divyesh.

'No,' said the voice. The same voice crackled on the intercom. He was covered completely with a full jacket-like garment, and his face had a cloth mask. As he spoke, the mask moved to his lines.

'That will not happen.'

That was his big mistake.

ॐ ✦ ॐ

Preziyan punched in the co-ordinates personally. Nobody else could be trusted with such a delicate mission.

He was at the computer center of the Labraska, formally christened the TIIZ (Technology and Intelligence Integration Zone). Fully stuffed with the most modern gizmos, the gadgets here were able to bring down an entire country's government system in half an hour. Heck, even Interpol's files were on their payroll list. The Mafia were truly all-pervading.

He was on their main computer, the Vilanova. This computer was the heart of TIIZ and the reason the Mafia did so well. Satellites, com-links, space ware, spyware, malware, telecom, and even VPN were nothing new.

Even the so-called blockchain technology was now theirs. The TIIZ was shaped like a Pentagon, a clever allusion to the Cold War period of the strife between Russia and the United States. The Pentagon was divided into three parts. System, tech, and designs. The system was all the internal workings of the Mafia, managing all the contacts of the Underworld, including finances.

Tech was the ultra-modern part of the TIIZ. Dedicated to new gadgets and innovative solutions, indigenously developed, or ingeniously stolen.

The design was Vilanova. A network of fifteen supercomputers, working constantly on ionic technology, the same technology used to power space flights. The fastest in existence and way more efficient.

Now, Preziyan cross-referenced the co-ordinates of the paper on Vilanova checking it with previous dealings, rather than actually checking the co-ordinates on the map. Why? Simple.

Troboyan Lazvensky was immaculately cultured, with security and subterfuge forming the basis of his hideouts. Recently, there have been rumors of a coordinated virus. A series of strings, numbers, and symbols were written in coordinate form but, when fed into the computer, rearranged themselves into one of the deadliest Trojan malwares ever. However, the Labraska transactions were virtually unrecognizable since everything was done TOR and Z-Space with the Russians. Moreover, Vilanova created a 62-character rotating cleartext every 15 seconds. It was virtually impossible for anything or anybody to guess sixty-two characters in 15 seconds to type in the passwords.

Preziyan was paranoid, but he decided to take a leap of faith. The first three came up blank. Such a place did not exist in the Mafia transaction system. And if it wasn't on their transaction system, it didn't exist in the world. Period.

However, the last one showed three hits. All three were from five to six years ago, for the Russian Mafia's stockpile of the S-400 Triumf surface-to-air missile. There were three names on that list.

Preziyan couldn't believe his eyes.

क◆र

The hooded one tapped his foot in quick succession in a secret code known to those loyal to the cause. He had now arrived at the main entrance of the place the ancients called the Other Room. Constructed by Atahualpa 6 years before his capture by the Spaniards, the hall was a startling contrast to his normal extravagance of silver and gold. Completely austere in its outlook, the hall was sparsely decorated, owing to the decline in Atahualpa's power, and it is this that was reflected in the making of the hall.

This was now the hideout. The final safe guide to Atahualpa's danger-ridden life, this hall served the council in the same fervor as before. The flame of truth was never meant to be hidden; it was meant to be proclaimed. Hernando Cortez had found that out the hard way when Peru showed zero resources but had incredible resistivity and resourcefulness. Homeranxtila was the throne name of Atahualpa, which supposedly, held the secret of the council. What it was, remains a mystery.

The massive iron-studded doors rumbled as a slit was opened in them, revealing an eccentric and crazy pair of eyes. Both were deathly silver, and the eyes looked like they could cut you down. And the hooded one knew from past experience that it certainly could. The eyes seemed to bore into him as if he could read his thoughts faster than they could form on his tongue. This was an ancient technique called iris-reading that only certain powerful sages could accomplish. And the fact that the eyes were set in was no less powerful.

'Ma Janegi Pramadofa Wamit Supnouna?' the faceless one asked.

'Pai. Inwasmet ti refinement.'

This was the legendary question asked by the secret guard of Atahualpa when questioning loyalty.

'Our loyalty is to the Inwasmet and the scroll.'

Meanwhile, to the Burning Flame, a quite amusing and dangerously beautiful demonstration was in progress. The chief, Batashyayi, opened the left sleeve of the suit. Concealed inside was a chip

'Ta-da! The first weapon. One-click and your enemy……,' he said, running his thumb across his throat.

Burning Flame had never really understood it.

'Explain. Give me a good demo. I am buying it.'

'Okay. I take this button inside my right bottom pocket and press. Chip flies out, turns into a 6 nano-bots and enters bloodstream of person. It can dictate any type of death in 30 seconds and come back to you. Recharge time of one and a half hours after 3 uses.'

'Which means just three good uses in high-speed combat,' the chief, Saud, continued.

'The next important point. Quick entry is only at close range. It cannot be fired more than 5 meters away. Have to see the opening. Eye, nostril, ears etc. also this movement must be subtle. Like slide of hand.'

Burning Flame showed why he wasn't needed for this part of the lecture with a smooth cut to the chief's stomach. Batashyayi doubled up, wheezing.

'Sorry…. sorry. Keep moving.'

'That's your first equipment. Quite handy if you ask me. Moving on, the next gizmo,' he said, opening up one button of the suit.

'Concealed inside this button is a scrambler. Eons ahead of its time, this beautiful piece of technology is actually a dual scrambler, which doesn't only intercept phone connections but also disrupts any satellite activity within 3 degrees of your position. All of this inside a button.'

The Burning Flame was impressed. Technology he hadn't ever seen or thought of. Now that wasn't something that happened every day. But there was something he needed to ask before the guy started speaking again. Surely, these pirates weren't smart enough to figure out the tech on their own. So, how did they get the info?

'Uh…. Batashyayi? Excuse me. Before we continue, simple question. How do you guys know all this? Who told it to you?' he asked, putting on his best investigative face.

Batashyayi was taken aback. Only two pieces into the suit, and the question arises. What luck.

'Sir, we captured a prisoner. A scientist onboard a ship. All the others, we killed in war. He was busy with this suit, so we rounded him up, brought him here, and made him spill. He says the suit is self-made, apparently,' he said, with the pride of a leader with the winning team.

Burning Flame couldn't care less. 'And which place is this guy from?'

Batashyayi now looked him in the eye, ready to throw it open.

'India.'

CHAPTER 8

Manco Inca was legend. He was make-believe. Thousands disapproved of his existence, and even more forbade checking. Manco Inca was beyond mere inquiries.

Known as the Death-Bringer, the Manco Inca was immensely powerful. Apparently well-versed in both the dark arts and golden magic,

He was the culmination of a deadly and catastrophic plan. There were rumors circulating that his mere stare could turn people to stone. More so, he was sometimes even rumored to have created dark rooms, or breakaways where he experimented potions and tried out new "powers." They said these dark rooms were the deadliest of places, for Manco Inca's presence was felt the most there.

There was another, darker, despicable reason these 'dark rooms' were made.

It was said that the Manco Inca turned prisoners of war into gold. Rumors and writings in some tests describe in great detail the way he dropped off their limbs, slicing them like he was sharpening his blade, and then how the water used to boil and froth at the ingestion of the prisoners. All of this time, Manco Inca would be in a trance, chanting parts of a powerful hymn to keep changing the of his potion. It was also said his worthier prisoners turned to lapis lazuli, his favorite jewel, to give them status.

This was simply a vault of the dead. Julianna was clearly reeling, and she fell down to the ground, unable to comprehend anything. She had arrived, completely by accident, at arguably the most sensational discovery of Manco Inca. His vault of the dead.

Now Julianna was face down, her eyes to the gold and lapis lazuli. Suddenly, she felt vibrations. Odd, unequal intervals. She looked up.

To her right, rocks were moving. A drum appeared out of the wall, and sticks beat it with a very old-fashioned pulley method.

The beating was growing louder each time, and the sound was deafening. As Julianna made sense of the Indiana Jones-like situation she now found herself in, she recalled reading something about a ritual in the Vaults. A gory, very vaguely understood ritual. She shuddered as she thought of the possibilities.

It was the call of the Prisoner.

The first name that popped up on the computer was:

Jorge Janismat. A Turkish businessman famous for his ships, he was one of the richest shipowners after the Greek Voyznus. The owner of 120 billion US dollars, totaling assets, and trade deals, he was quite the jackpot. And he had some kind of connection with Troboyan. But what was it? Ships? He needed to check it out.

Prys Danckinson. The Dutch aviation billionaire was the ex-owner of Gulfstream Jets Corp before moving on to be a shareholder in Bombardier, along with stakes in Airbus, Boeing, and Dassault Aviation. There was no doubt that this guy was in contact with some big fish. Yet again, Troboyan didn't fit. Hedge fund transfers, maybe? He wasn't sure. Maybe flights were a necessity at the point of intersection.

And the final name.

Francesco Garibaldini. The acclaimed Argentine food maestro, he was a chef well sought after for his schnitzel napolitana, among his other famous delicacies. A master of the culinary arts, Garibaldi defied cookbooks and decades of cultural restrictions to bring his own variations, often adding unheard of ingredients for experiments. His chicken roast with Indian curry was a world-famous example.

And yet again, Troboyan couldn't have added him just for culinary chagrin. He was involved somehow.

Putting down his pen, he looked at the three names once again. It was utterly impossible to detect any similarity between them in any facet whatsoever. However, Troboyan Lazvensky was a recurring theme. Why? No point of cross-reference was mentioned.

What was the need for Troboyan to seek them out?

೫ ✦ ಞ

Divyesh was used to machismo, big time. There wasn't any effect of the terrorist's comment on him. He had learned control incredibly early in his life, and he wasn't about to let go anytime soon.

However, he did have an extremely low tolerance for bullshit.

Bong! On the head. The gun was dropped, the syringe he held onto. Wham! Another neat and nice knock to the crotch. Complete serfdom now. Syringe down, gun down. Divyesh placed both in his rucksack and took to unboxing the parcel he just received.

The mask was made of cloth, so it unraveled quickly, all the way, till his eyes had a clear vision. A golden yellow pair of contact lenses were visible, and it had this intense scorching look to it, when combined with the eyes it was set upon. More unraveling revealed his nose, which was beak like and protruding out.

He was just about to get to the bottom half of his face when Divyesh's opponent finally made his move.

He had timed it well.

The cloth blocked Divyesh's peripheral vision, so it was impossible for him to see the leg jab out at his shins. Caught him fair and square. Divyesh groaned and stumbled for a second. That time proved its worth for the man as he used his cloth to rewrap his face and quickly position himself again.

Divyesh suddenly dropped low and, using an old trick he learned at RAW, feigned his shoulder, moving to the left. The masked assailant, anticipating the move from the left, changed his stance to put his right foot forward, turning his body toward to Divyesh's left. And he fell right into the trap.

Grappling the man's leg, he buckled it upwards and kicked the other leg hard enough for it to crack, immediately creating a suction downwards. The man fell down unconscious due to internal hemorrhaging due to a hit from his own knee.

Tired, Divyesh put down the body and sat down.

'Is there anyone else?'

౫✦ಇ

'Take me to him!' Burning Flame said.

What use was talking to the got when the lion's share was inside, flush for the take?

Batashyayi obliged.

So he wound up the staircase that had mysteriously appeared with the quiet swiveling of the bookcase forming the backdrop of Batashyayi's chair.

There was a door every 64 steps. One was labeled 'Missiles,' another 'grenades,' and so on. After what seemed like five lifetimes but was actually 1024 steps, they arrived at door no 16.

'Prisoners,' it said.

'Nefertiti, give me the keys,' said Batashyayi to a comrade beside him. Keys passed over; a minute was spent in silence as the chief of the Somalian pirates fumbled with the plethora of keys at his disposal. Finally finding the right one, he nodded to Burning Flame and slotted in the key. He turned it slowly, clearly for effect.

Once opened, the room showed a very grisly sight. It was very small, about just twelve or fourteen square feet. A two-by-two tap was present, and a blanket was thrown on the floor, unwashed and peeling away.

There were no windows.

In one corner sat the object of interest, the prisoner they had come to see.

The prisoner held in his hand a miniature flute, symbolic of the ones used by so many in India.

And he was smiling.

ॐ ✦ ☘

Preziyan's mind was whizzing. Never had such a case ever happened before. Moreover, the government had specifically requested the solving of the case. Being on the right side of the government was the right trump card, so the job had to be done.

He checked the date of the three entries separating each one from oldest to newest client. This is what came up.

Danckinson – 24/5/2011

Janismat – 5/2/2010

Garibaldini – 3/6/2009

So Garibaldini was their oldest client. But Gribalsini was a chef, wasn't he? He knew the Russian Mafia never really did question a client's motives when buying a product, but this was too weird, even by their standards. What recipe could a chef possibly concoct with a fucking missile? Unless…

Preziyan thought for a few minutes. And then he closed Vilanova, plugged off the SB and walked by coolly to Daniel's room.

At the same time, 16000 kilometers away in Buenos Aries, Argentina, one man watched his computer start hacking into the Russian Mafia's internal servers.

His name was Garibaldini.

CHAPTER 9

The professor pulled up her spectacles as she looked at the posse of students seated at the corner of the lecture hall.

'Now, young man, just how would you explain what you had been doing?' she asked, fingers pointed directly at the brusque young man who was garnering attention for quite some while now.

'I was surfing, Ma'am,' said the guy, who went by the name of Johannes. He had, in fact, been using his phone to check the stability of a D2 Hydrogen bomb.

'What were you surfing on the web for, Johannes? And this is neither the time nor the place for it!'

'I apologize, Ma'am.'

'Out, boy. And a repeat offense in my class will mean you become the next janitor.'

Johannes picked up his bag to the jeering of all except a few. He wasn't welcome, and he knew it. But everybody was. That is until they do something that people will respect them for.

This was the second time he had been kicked out. He really needed to control his emotions, or his aims and ambitions could be put at risk. He knew the thread he was dangling by, and he knew that the thread could be broken anytime, any day.

He kicked a can as he made his way through the garden to the university gates. Flashing his I-card, he quickly got onto his motorbike and sped out, glancing at the plaque stuck on the stone walls before gunning his engines.

The plaque read Yale University.

ဢ ✦ ಞ

The man was slowly brought into the hall. The chamber was essentially a subterranean crypt, having been built for burial purposes. However, it had been the ruling of the Sapas that this place be converted. The hall was covered regally in the glory of the lost Incan treasures, along with frescos of common life adorning the walls. The community had been living so far from their homeland ever since that man Hiram Bingham had stumbled upon it.

Their secrecy was threatened, and they moved to the relative safety of Vietnam, but the US- Vietnam conflict-hit out at them. In spite of all odds, they had survived. They could pass on the message. They could fulfill the last wish of the Sapa Inca. They were the Guardians.

And now, the time had come to set in motion a series of events that would, at last, bring out the truth. And he was to be a part of it.

He slowly turned his head to the raised platform in front of him. Present in front of him were five thrones. On each throne, a member of the High Council. These men were the all-accomplished ones, the left and right-hand of the Sapa Inca. Each one garnered their own respect, as each one was a master of the five realms of the Incan civilization. War, astrology, elemental sciences, maths, and the dark arts.

But it was the throne in the center that was the highlight. Sitting royally on it was a man of about forty. Elegantly dressed in a double overcoat and jeans, he wore the traditional Inca crown, a bronze, jade, and lapis lazuli marvel.

This man was referred to as Anxtila. Nobody knew his past or his upbringing. Of course, all your past identities were shunned when you entered the High Council.

But Anxtila was different. This man attracted attention wherever he went. His aquiline jaw and intelligent, seeing eyes gave you the impression that he knew more than he was telling you.

That is precisely why nobody dared contradict him.

Suddenly, the messenger bowed low, so low that his head almost touched the ground. Rocking his head back and forth, he beat his chest five times, opening and closing his hand with each beat.

Courtesy call done, he then knelt down and finally faced the Lord. Heart beating, veins popping, he awaited the verdict that the Lord would give. But there was none.

'Pahwani!' he said. 'Speak!'

'My Lord,' he said, continuing in the ancient tongue. 'The British lady found the first of the dark rooms. There is a chance she would have deciphered the first.'

'How?'

'Uh... my Lord, my Nobaijita is gone.'

'Your Nobaijita is gone? What happened? Did it just bloody disappear or did the Manco Inca himself steal it?' the Lord asked, anger rising with each word.

'The Nobaijita, the K is the most important link. How could you?' he asked, collapsing back into his throne.

He had to cool down his mind before he could think. What were the worst-case scenarios? The British would have found the stone. But they couldn't decipher it, could they?

Heaving a sigh of relief, he looked back at the messenger. However, for starters, there were some loose ends that needed to be tied up.

ഇ ✦ ൱

Divyesh went inside the cockpit and restored it to sanity. After that, it was pretty much a normal flight for him. Of course, being the hero, the people were anything were normal.

Touching down at Copenhagen International, the hijackers were loaded up and packed for Interpol. Meanwhile, Divyesh made his way over to the immigration counters. Standing in a huge queue, he tried to pass the time by guessing the nationalities of the people near him. He saw passports that looked Ecuadorian, he adjudged a French couple correctly, and he also identified the blue of the United Nation's passport.

'Next!' a voice shouted. Divyesh looked back to see that counter number twelve was beckoning him, having just completed the last check.

Divyesh rambled on slowly, pulling out his passport and flight ticket. The Ashoka Chakra and the Sarnath symbol on the passport reaffirmed the fact that he was, indeed, a citizen of India.

'Passport, please,' grumbled the official. It was easy to guess that this guy was not happy with work.

After returning the passport, customary questions such as 'What is your purpose for visiting?' were asked, and Divyesh was waved into the baggage collection areas.

'Thanks,' he said. The official only gave a small, wavering smile in return. Somehow, Divyesh didn't like that smile. It wasn't very reassuring, and it made him feel uneasy, like something was going to happen. Something that was going to alter his present state, shake him by the roots and fix him back again.

He just didn't know when and what.

ಋ ✦ ಞ

Walking toward the prisoner, Burning Flame felt but one thing in his mind: unease. He was an experienced dealer, having been in a myriad of deals with the eclectic Somalis before. In this long 'career,' he had seen many an extraordinary person and things. So much so that he had even been instrumental in hitting out and toppling entire governments for his needs.

But nothing in all that experience prepared him for this prisoner. He was different somehow. His body had been beaten to a pulp, but somehow, his eyes conveyed something different. They were sharp and crystal clear, a kind of pathway to the gem of a mind within.

Slowly moving toward the prisoner, he hit him to wake him up, although he seemed awake. The prisoner shook his head, and his eyes slowly focused on a man. He took one look and started muttering something.

'Huh? What was that? I didn't catch that,' said Burning Flame.

He moved closer to hear what the prisoner was saying. He heard just one word repeated over and over again.

'Dhanwantri…Dhanwantri…Dhanwantri…'

Chapter 10

The Incans were very particular about security. It was a belief that once life began, everything in it had to be safeguarded so that their most prized possession could be taken into the afterlife.

At the top of that list was their city. The main reason for Macchu Picchu's existence was not just a political stronghold but a spiritual seat. It was symbolic of their success. Their greatness.

They had gone to great lengths to keep their secrets safe from outsiders. The secrets, the money that the treasury contained, the harem, everything was safely tucked away from prying eyes. But you could never be too sure.

Of course, they had their own counter measures. Julianna had heard of fire breathing serpents that opened their mouths to cast forth jets of fire, poison arrows that were fabled to be shot just once but would never miss their target, after which the invaders had to cross what was called Manco Inca's 'Pit of devotion.'

A huge pit of burning acid, a huge expanse of acid that could have spanned an entire cavern, needed to be crossed. The only way to do so was by using a rope bridge that the Incans had affixed to the wall.

Easy, right? No.

The rope bridges were present, but they could only be taken out by inserting a specially-made slab that just fit into the hole. Upon turning it, the rope bridge could be taken out and used.

Where was the stone? Nobody knew. Only the Sapa Inca was privy to the knowledge, and he was dead five thousand years ago. But all this was if the invaders decided to actually invade.

Exactly at the place Julianna stood, there was a mechanism so ahead of its time that its concept was considered alien.

A pressure pad.

A smooth mound of rock had been placed at the center of the dark room. Moving it even a quarter of an inch away from its position would trigger an avalanche of rocks and marbles coming in through the only possible method: the doorway.

The victim was trapped inside and effectively crushed to death.

This was the call of the Prisoner.

How did the rocks come about? The rock was connected by a thread to a mechanism that resembled a trapdoor. These trapdoors were present along the sides of the doorway. Concealed behind the trapdoor were lots and lots of rocks. These trapdoors were opened when the strings were pulled tight, i.e., when the stone was moved from its position. There was no way to undo it.

Julianna felt this entire information course through her as she decided her next step. She had to take her legs off the stone, even if it meant starting an avalanche. Because the fact of the matter was that she couldn't stay here, could she? There was a chance it wouldn't move.

The drumbeats didn't help either.

Her heart was beating, and she slowly very slowly took her left foot off the rock and slowly placed it on the ground. No movement. The next leg was the trick. Applying too much pressure would move the rock, and the pressure difference created by removing the leg might also move it.

Julianna improvised. She lifted up her heel, almost as high as when a ballerina performs, and removed her foot with an angle that was perpendicular to the rock. She kept her foot down. No sound.

Sighing contentedly, she turned. As she was turning, her right heel brushed against the stone, wobbling it very slightly. The sounds of the stone shaking were audible to her. Julianna froze.

She waited. Nothing happened. Sensing victory, she took another step. No sooner had she done it than a single sound hit her hand.

Zip!

The trapdoors had opened.

像 ✦ ఒ

Johannes slowly turned his bike inside the garage. As he did so, he pulled out his phone and made a quick call to Rufais. He picked up on the second ring.

'Hello? Rufais? Yeah, I'm back home. Call the hatchback to the rendezvous.'

Rufais, on the other hand, was in the middle of an argument.

'Uh dude, can I call you later? I'm in, like, the middle of an intense fight scene, bruh,' he said.

'Okay. Fine then.'

What could the fight be about that would prompt Rufais to refuse to answer the rendezvous call?

Anyways a quick turnaround brought about the familiar smell of home for Johannes. His home, his refuge, his last resort.

He walked toward the doors of the house. There was no keyhole. The doors looked like slabs of stone just placed there.

But then, Johannes didn't have a conventional key.

Johannes brought out his hands from his jacket pocket. He placed his palm about a meter from the center of the doors. From his palms, an electromagnetic pulse was emitted to the backside of the door.

Behind the door existed the marvel. A conversion machine, he called it. It converted real, live objects into mere holograms and vice versa. It worked on electromagnetic induction of the 'engines' inside it. Making the door a hologram, Johannes passed through, entering into… another world.

The house was indeed otherworldly, to say the least. It had the very same interior design as an inspired UFO, with curved circular walls and compact-sized spacing. Directly in front was a long, winding staircase that led up to the first floor. On the left, one was greeted by a pair of rooms; doors painted bright white, labeled 'Panel Room' and 'Mains Room.' Moving further along the left side of the hall would reveal the kitchen, a huge, open wonder done up in a setting taking inspiration from both the Chinese and Indian cultures. The kitchen was arranged in the form of concentric circles, complete with a stove at the center and a conveyor belt forming the last circle, making it look like a sushi bar.

On the right-hand side, the first three rooms were marked 'confidential.' This was merely a decoy as the rooms were just filled with closets. However, with the work Johannes was involved in, he couldn't take risks.

Again, moving your eyes away from the nearest room would show you the entrance to a really plush and well laid out garden, adjacent to which were an Olympic sized swimming pool, and a fairly well-equipped gym. His bedrooms and guest quarters were in a rather unassuming building behind the gym.

Ignoring all this, Johannes immediately took to the steps, reaching the first floor, which only consisted of four rooms in total.

The first one was his room, which he just didn't bother opening. His room was sparsely decorated, and you could draw a parallel to Julian Assange's residence at the Ecuadorian embassy, save for the magnified size of the room.

The second was his parents' room. That room didn't exist anymore. It did, until the dad decided to run off, leaving the 11-year-old kid with his mom. His mother worked hard and put herself through hell to get him through college. Shortly after, God felt her life's duty was complete, and she passed on as well.

In that room, there were very few memories that Johannes' parents ever existed: their photos, letters, journals, and some clothes. He hardly ever bothered with it.

The third room was the rendezvous room. This room was the cradle of their rejuvenation, the mother of all their ideas, their incubation sphere. The room contained stacks upon stacks of files, all from different hatch-ups that they had come with it. As he remembered, the blackboard would still be fresh with the points of the last discussion still etched on it.

The walls would contain newspaper clippings. Of what, you might ask. Of articles related to what they wanted to accomplish. Now comes the million-dollar question. What were they trying to accomplish?

The answer lied in a tattoo on his arm. Annuit Coeptus. The famous line from the United States' dollar bill caught his imagination at a young age and then secret societies became something of a passion. He wanted to explore, to figure out their mysteries. Johannes had once contemplated an application to join, but circumstances didn't quite allow him to.

Out of all the secret societies in the world, Johannes loved the Freemasons. They were the most liberal, with most meetings being public knowledge and also partly due to the fabulous wealth they possessed. This room was covered in research work about Masonry and other 'shady' organizations.

Now, to the last room. This room was special because it was never opened. The builder who built his house had warned Johannes that if he opened the door, his life would never be the same again. Johannes loved his life, and hence, he resisted the urge to open the door.

He was on his way to his room when a faint 'twang' was heard.

Johannes immediately dropped low, positioning himself into a fighting stance similar to the Shaolin monks. You see, his dad might have been a bad person, but he sure did teach him how to fight.

The twang? Simple. A tripwire. No matter how advanced the house was, the crudest safety measure was sometimes the most effective, as was proved by this episode.

He fell deathly silent as a shadow of a man swept up the wall, and his long boots could be heard trampling the stairs. Slowly, a figure began to materialize.

Completely covered, he was wearing a long dress, symbolic of the dishdasha worn by the Arabs, and carried with him a huge lead-lined suitcase that looked completely impenetrable.

He came up the flight of stairs and slowly removed his headrest, putting down his suitcase. Johannes was still crouched, his arms and legs ready to pounce for an immediate attack. A bald head came into view, followed by a beard that, combined with the facial features, resembled a man he well recognized.

'Dad?!'

ഇൗ ✦ ଓ

The ancients looked upon the buildings as a gateway to success. Success not just in this life, but in the life beyond. There existed a realm that was a kind of purgatory for souls, judging them for their deeds and choosing whether they get sent to Heaven or Hell. They also believed that specific structures gave people express access into this realm. Foremost among them were the pyramids.

The Rosicrucians built huge replicas of these pathways to the nether realm in Pennsylvania, USA. The order of the Oriental Temple (Ordo Templi Orientalis) and the Freemasons all revered the sacred structure, for they understood its power.

However, it all started with the rise of one empire: the Egyptians. Believed to have been the longest-ruling empire ever, the Pantheon of Egyptian Gods strongly reflected their people's belief in massive constructions. Hieroglyphics adorn the walls of these wonders of ancient technology that inspire amazement in modern scholars. The original architects, the Egyptians, believed that the pyramids were steps to heaven, and that is why the temple at

Abu Simbel and the Pyramids of Giza were all made with a topmost stone, a capstone. The pyramids needed the capstone to become the symbol of the higher power, and hence, the capstone completion was the embodiment of Egyptian devotion to the powers above. Similar to the cornerstone ceremony of the Freemasons, the ceremony of the capstone was a religious practice, taken very seriously to appease both the pharaohs and the Gods.

That being said, there was still a burgeoning doubt. If the pyramids were held in such high regard, and were a symbol of the eternal power, would it be reduced to just a burial site for the kings and their families. No. there must be something more. Something beyond the blocks of stone, something beneath all that rubble.

And it was just waiting to be discovered.

Chapter 11

'What are your thoughts on Garibaldini's orders? Do you think we should have sold it to him?'

Preziyan and Daniel were in the latter's residence. And Preziyan was being pressed vigorously on his action and the subsequent consequences.

'Sir, with all due respect, how is it that a cook could acquire such advanced military intelligence? Moreover, he was just a cook. What was he going to do with it? Fire up his kitchen?'

'Then tell me, Preziyan. How do I refuse him? A client is a client. And we are businessmen. Bottom line.'

Preziyan knew he had to give it more time to get past Daniel's quick fixes.

'Here's the thing, boss. Troboyan had those co-ordinates and running it brought out Garibaldini as the oldest client for us. Naturally, he serves as one of the main customers which leaves only two possibilities to consider.'

'And they are?' Daniel asked.

'Well, here is one. He had been linked to some military facility in Argentina, on contract, I guess. But then again, given his position, what could he have done? The added trouble is we know nothing about his past or present status.

'What? That cannot be. Did you check the records?'

Daniel was utterly shocked.

The fact is, no trade is ever done with complete assurance in both the buyer and seller's minds. And the Mafia were no exception.

Every single client of the Mafia was deeply scrutinized and thoroughly checked, and only after that were they even allowed to make a proposition. Financial status, marital status, property, jobs, associates, medical reports, and anything else related to the person were all recorded and kept in the Mafia's archives, should a time arise when they needed those details again, for a different purpose.

Of course, there was always a question of variables. What would happen if the facts changed? A simple address change or something more complex?

The fact of the matter was that the Russians never really left their clients. Even if it was a one-off deal, they were a client. Hence, there is a need to keep an eye on them. And if the Russian Mafia was well-known for anything, it was their incredible network of spies and informants.

Unfortunately, in Garibaldini's case, there had been a mishap. The address on his file had said Rosario, Argentina. He had been born and brought up there. They had proof in the fact that Garibaldini swore allegiance to Newell's Old Boys, and that was proof enough.

Now was a different story. Preziyan's eyes and ears had given him reports of him staying in Buenos Aires, renting a house, buying a car. Of course, all this could have been faked, but the network never lied. Obviously, the visuals helped as well.

After all, what couldn't the Mafia do? A few simple taps on the computer board gave them access to all the CCTVs placed ubiquitously under the banner of 'Safety' and 'protection' of the nation. However, shifting through the many terabytes of data was obviously a herculean task.

Failures aplenty, they finally struck gold on an intersection camera that overlooked the parliament. A clear shot of Garibaldini getting out of a car, a 1998 Cadillac, and going into the main gate of the Secretary's office.

That had confirmed his suspicions. Something was not right with Garibaldini. He had changed his address to a different one in Buenos Aires. But why? There had to be some motive.

He was just about to voice his thoughts when a sudden red alert echoed through the building.

Vilanova!

ಕ ◆ ಞ

Divyesh slowly made his way to the mass of waiting placards that bombarded the exit of the airport, carefully reading each card to find out his name.

But neither did his name come, nor his man.

He moved out of the exit and walked over to a taxi stand that stood imposingly on the walkway.

'Hi, I would like a taxi,' he asked.

The man sitting at the counter looked up.

'What?'

'I would like a taxi.'

'Where to?'

Divyesh pulled out the small envelope that had arrived as part of the package the Defense Ministry had sent him. On it was the insignia of the Defense Ministry, along with their saying:

'When you are one among a million and one in a million.'

Those words always filled Divyesh with pride. The risks one had to take to be so, starting all the way from school.

First, the NCC, then the special corps, and then finally, the entry into the NDA. The National Defense Academy.

This was the pride of the nation. This was where the babies littered and turned into real men. They morphed, they changed, and they evolved. For the better. To be at the frontiers of their country.

Anyways, back to the present. He opened the envelope. Out came a light blue paper with a single line printed on it.

"Here. This is where I want to go," he said, and he handed the paper to the man.

The man took the paper and stared at it hard. A frown crept up on his face as he replied in a heavily accented North-Eastern European English, 'this place… I can't drive you inside.'

'Huh? What did you say?' said Divyesh, as he wasn't expecting that answer.

'I mean, any cab in Denmark cannot get you there.'

'You mean you can't reach this place in a cab?'

'No. you go there personally. They wouldn't let me in.'

'Right. Can I have the paperback?'

Divyesh took the paperback. And on it, in neatly embossed letters, were written two words.

Rosenborg Palace.

ॐ ✦ ॐ

Burning Flame was thoroughly done with this prisoner. He was proving to be far more resilient than any other prisoner he had ever dealt with.

At the time, the prisoner had been going through a medieval torture method called the chair. It had been very successful during the Spanish Inquisition, and Burning Flame was a fan.

It consisted of a chair, obviously of the reclining kind, that extended a portion of its legs forward at the touch of a lever, almost making it a bed. The process was slow, so the legs moved up one at a time.

Nice and easy, right? If only.

Each inch of the chair was covered with sharp spikes, almost twenty centimeters in length. Being that long, it was meant to bring pain, not death. At the end of the armrest, there was a small motorable blade. This meant it could move between the fingers, cutting them one by one, again and again, with the whole process ironically being controlled by hand.

The legs of the chair, however, were different. They were made of iron, just smooth iron with a small socket-like opening at the apex. Through this hole, one would pour through a choice of the most corrosive acids in the world: Nitric acid, sulphuric acid and even the famed Aqua Regia, the acid that could dissolve the sacred gold. Slowly hitting on the iron, it would dissolve it with the afterburns on the legs. The legs, once raised, would move slowly for effect.

This would move the acid around while also putting pressure on the pelvic area being pierced by the spikes. It was an absolute abomination, a punishment that even the worst monsters wouldn't wish on their enemies. Its use was banned very early on for the sake of humanity.

But Burning Flame wasn't really keen on being humane. He just wanted information.

'Tell me! Just tell me, and this pain ends now, he said once again to the prisoner.

'I…no... don't know…. job… protect…secrets of this…. Thing,' the prisoner rambled, spitting out a huge patch of blood even as he felt the throat get pierced.

'Tell me! Talk now, you little bitch!'

'I……..no…. leave me!' came out of the prisoners mouth, as a passing whisper.

'Well, just die then, OR TELL ME WHAT I WANT TO KNOW!!'

Burning Flame was about to do the unthinkable when the prisoner suddenly spoke.

'Parma…. Parmanu….,' he said as his body went limp.

'Huh? What? What was that,' he asked, only to be greeted by silence in return.

'Okay, boys, wrap it up then. Parmanu. That is what he said, yes? We have got what we wanted then!'

Batashyayi couldn't believe it. This man had just literally flung the prisoner aside like a ragdoll with no regard for his life. All this for a single word? His humanity was non-existent, it seemed.

'Batashyayi! Did you hear me? We need to go. Wrap it up.'

CHAPTER 12

She heard the roar, before she could register what was happening. It was a deafening sound, thousands of rocks hurtling through the doorway, waiting to take precisely what Julianna was clinging on to. Her life.

Julianna saw the avalanche coming and immediately strategized. Perfectly oval rocks and a first glance did not reveal any abnormalities. Her heart rate was increasing, and it was becoming very hard for her to keep thinking with a cool head.

She willed herself to calm down and breathe. One. Two. Then she ran her eyes around again. There! This time, she saw something. A small crack, with light spewing through it at the northeast corner of the room.

She quickly ran toward it and pushed away from the rocks covering the crack. She was astonished to find a tunnel, pitch black, leading downwards.

She looked back one last time. The first rocks had reached, they were within her eyesight. Quickly, squeezing her body, she closed the rock just as the first rock hurtled against the room. She then took out her torchlight from her breast pocket and switched it on. Immediately, a beam of light hit the floor.

Safe, she now looked at the flight of oddly fashioned stairs on which were sketched various figures of the Incan way of life. Moving down one step at a time, she could see each step had a different activity for the Incans. One showed body-building, the next an impression of jewelry making, an art the Incans excelled at, and so on.

The truth did not strike her until she came onto a break into the steps from where it went down further. There on the rock was engraved a scene of the King walking down these precise steps.

Then she got it. This was the royal tunnel, a chamber tunnel connecting the three main centers of Incan royalty: Cuzco, Macchu Picchu and Ollantaytambo, the super fortress that Manco Inca had built in his reign to serve as an indestructible hideout.

As she moved up her torch to the ceiling, a sudden painting caught the light of her torch. Not believing her eyes, she focused the light onto the picture, not comprehending the reason for its existence here.

It was an Ouroboros. A serpent eating its own tail symbolized a circle of completeness, albeit with hate and insanity. The Ouroboros was a dark symbol, no doubt, and its presence on the arms of the members of the now-famous Illuminati served as a reminder of but one thing:

Suffering.

Julianna had heard of the Illuminati and the Ouroboros but never associated it with the Incas.

It was only as she went ever further below that she would come to know how much; just how much she didn't know.

഼ ✦ ഼

There had been a breach of Vilanova! This couldn't be happening. This was, all odds considered, very close to impossible.

Quickly leaving Daniel's room, the duo made their way over to TIIZ, their hearts getting heavier, piling up with the weight of their worries.

Entering the facility, they found total pandemonium. Vilanova was beeping the heads off the scientists, all the while pointing to about fifty red spots as potential threats to the Mafia. It was but obvious that this was not a random attack. Someone, something had triggered it.

'What the hell just happened?' asked Daniel to one of the technicians.

'We don't know, sir. Vilanova just seemed to spontaneously break down. I know this is bad, but the initial diagnosis, and my sneaking suspicion, might be that Vilanova is the victim of a …. Hack.'

Daniel went berserk.

'DO YOU THINK I FUCKING PAY FOR YOUR SUSPICIONS? GET ON WITH FIXING IT! YOUR OPINION ISN'T GOING TO SET IT RIGHT! THIS IS MY DREAM, AND IT'S IN RUINS! FIX IT!'

The technician scurried away, muttering something about the inevitability of his fate. Daniel turned to Preziyan, whose face had turned deep red, almost beetroot-like, and he seemed to be past despair, almost in a state of self-reflection.

'What's wrong with you? Let's go and find out what happened.'

'Uh. Daniel,' he began.

'What?'

'I think I know the reason for this mess.'

Daniel was stumped.

'You do? And you didn't tell me all this time? Really?'

'Uh…. you see….,' and he told him about the thought he had before entering in the co-ordinates.

'A what? A coordinate virus? Preziyan, how could you be so insanely foolish?'

'You know the struggles I had to endure, the sacrifices I made, and the promises I broke just to build Vilanova. I have murdered thirteen people, not one, not two, but thirteen people for Vilanova. And unless you can fix this fucking shitstorm, I promise you, it will be 14.'

Preziyan honestly had no idea what to do. The boss was completely in rage mode.

'Daniel, I'm going to get my best technicians on the job. I am sorry for the screw-up,' he added, genuinely feeling regret.

'Is there any fucking point?' Daniel remarked, disappointment written all over his face. And that was enough for Preziyan.

"I am doing this myself, boss. I will bring back Vilanova to her glory, and I will bring back the head of the scumbag that did this. I give you, my word."

ॐ ✦ ௳

He couldn't believe his eyes. 'Dad?' he exclaimed, unable to comprehend his reason for arrival. Almost instantly, his mind began a sweep of the imposing man in front of him to check for any threats. Force of habit.

He carried a suitcase. The body looked way too taut for his clothes. So there was a possibility of a weapon, at most a Magnum 22, but chances where he had come empty-handed. However, Johannes didn't rely on chance.

Hundreds of questions came through his mind, and he chose to ask the most general one first, funneling into the specifics.

"What are you doing here? Why did you come here? After so many years? You left us, right? Why did you come? To fuck me up again?"

The man just smiled, lips parting to reveal a voice. A voice deeply magnified yet soothing in nature, like a thunderstorm that seeks to cleanse, not destroy.

"Heh... tch. So many questions, son. I'll answer all of them. I haven't come here to damage your life, so please stop having these preconceived ideas."

Johannes turned his head in disgust. The man pretended not to see it.

'What am I doing here? Simple. I came here to save you. As for why I left you and your mother, it was in your best interest. Your mother promised to me on her deathbed that she wouldn't tell you my identity and that I should promise to tell it to you myself when the time was right.'

'So what are you waiting for? Show me who you are, Dad,' he said, repressed contempt fueled into the last word.

'Not so soon, son. Not so soon. I see you are agitated, not in the right state of mind. Okay then. Maybe when you're ready. Until then, keep this for me,' he said, handing over an ornately covered package, cubical in shape, into Johannes' hand.

'Huh?' was all that Johannes could manage.

'Son. Be ready. We don't have much time. I mean it. The next time we meet, I might not have this luxury. Understand. Change, and you will be enlightened,' said the man. And then, without missing a beat, the man left, running back down the very same stairs he had been on a moment ago, barely giving Johannes any time to register his leaving.

Nothing of what just happened made the tiniest amount of sense to Johannes. But he had concrete proof. The cubical package. His hand quickly went over to undo the package, but his gut feeling told him this wasn't the time. He didn't understand what it was, but his mind told him to exercise caution.

Johannes took the package and went inside his room, placing it on the table. As he did, he noticed a small note addressed to him attached to the bottom.

"For you, my son. Hope you get the opportunity to open it when the time is right. Love, Dad."

One couldn't ignore the fact that the heat in the Middle East was of dizzying proportions. It was very hard for people to live here, and yet the Egyptian civilization were able to unite the passage to Africa with the Middle East, and further this place was bought to its glory by a group of people known for their intricate stone carvings and also, their art of deception.

The Nabatiyans.

These people ruled over what was present-day Jordan, parts of Syria, Palestine, and even as far as Aswan in Egypt. Controlling the established caravan route, the pull of business by luring travelers to rest in their city gave them some much-needed fame.

And their strategic location meant easy alliances.

But all that lies now is rubbish. The real reason was survival. Since the advent of time, man has always looked for comfy solutions to life.

Two thousand years ago, the rocky landscape that the eyewitnesses today would have been replaced by a completely opposite feature. Lush green forests, with flowing rivers all around, ensure their food, water, and shelter.

Migrating, they set up a civilization, eventually gaining a name like no other in the Arab Continent. They did not merely just set up cities or towns, but they drew upon their immense engineering skills and sketched a city so beautiful that its praises would be sung for eons.

The city of Petra.

Chapter 13

Denmark's capital, Copenhagen is a compact city that contains a spicy, yet relaxed atmosphere. Though it has a well-established culture and tradition, Copenhagen keeps progressing. It blends its old-world charm and cosmopolitan outlook to create a crafty concoction of elegance and modernism. Filled with resplendent royal attractions, Divyesh truly believed Copenhagen had something for everyone.

And he was now on his way to see one of their most amazing structures.

Four hundred years of splendor and royal cadence is captured in the Rosenborg Palace. It was built by Christian the Fourth in the seventeenth century. It served as the residence of the royals of Denmark.

Built up in a stunning Gothic composition and ancient archaic elements of Greece, Rosenborg Palace stood out as an ode to the traditionalist beauty of Denmark while the rest of the country embraced the modern side of architecture and culture, and this juxtaposition symbolized the harmony of the state.

As they say, opposite poles do attract, for in truth, part of Denmark's allure could be traced back to this very confluence.

The taxi came to a stop about 25 meters from his destination. 'Sorry. This is as far as I can go, he said.

'That would be 50 euros, please.'

Divyesh handed him the money and got out of the cab with his briefcase clinging to him.

As he looked around, he noticed people in suits, mostly bankers by the look of them, moving about the street showcasing a wide range of stresses on their face. Some walking with clenched fists and some banging the pavement in frustration. Nobody was as chill as Divyesh, and in that sense, he attracted a lot of attention to himself.

At this point in time, his team at RAW had managed to get into his apartment to try and get a sense of his whereabouts. Madhav had already disabled voice recognition and was onto figuring a way around the iris scanner.

Suddenly, Sunil received a call alert. He opened up his phone (a flip phone, yes) and saw it was from the Defense Ministry. He took it.

'Hello, Sir? How are you? I hope everything is fine?'

'Yeah Sunil. No time for small talk, however. Don't try and break into Divyesh's apartment. He is on deputation with us in Denmark now. After he finishes his mission, he will come back to you. Until then, you may have to adjust,' said the Minister, in a manner sounding like an order, not a request.

'But how could you send him before telling us? Is that fair, sir? Our work is incredibly important, and you know that all too well,' said Sunil, careful to keep his anger in check.

'When did I ever say that your work wasn't important? Anyway, I can't go on with this. You have got to make do with this until Divyesh comes. That's it. Jai hind.'

'Sir, sir! Impossible!' Screamed Sunil as the call disconnected. He turned to his team, which was working furiously.

'Guys, stop, stop! He isn't here!'

Raghav perked up.

'What? Where is he now?'

'On deputation with the Defense Ministry, apparently. In Denmark.'

There was silence for a few minutes. Everybody had but one thought in their minds. Only Hafeez managed to voice it out.

'Shit!'

॑❖ಒ

Outside, John and Stacy employ every method in the book to find some crevices and some openings to find Julianna. So much drilling had happened, about sixteen hours of it, in a World Heritage site. And yet, no sign of her had been found. It seemed the earth wanted to lose Julianna in her chasms, away from the pull of the world.

But they wouldn't give up so easily. They brought in a sensor to try to detect which part of the ground was hollow. But it was as if the ground had reformed itself after Julianna's fall. It had been sixteen days since they last saw Julianna. Being a UNESCO site, only one hour of drilling was permitted, in the best interests of both governments. Hence, progress was pretty slow. There had been the thought of blasting through to speed up the process, but for fear of global backlash over the quite possibly irreversible damage of a world-renowned monument, that plan had been shelved.

How else would they then find her? The sensors were still working their way through the rock, and there remained precisely 10 minutes before the authorities would shoo today's attempt away. They had to cover as much ground as possible. After all, how long could this go on for?

John looked at Stacy as worry lines stretched her young face.

'It isn't that far away, Stace. She is close by. I just know it.'

Stacy, however, being the more practical of the two, did not have that much faith.

'How much longer, John? I fear the worst. I have already received calls from Downing Street trying to talk me out of these attempts. What am I to do? Just look at the position we are in. Even Julianna's, for that matter. She came to find something, and she got lost. Literally. The fucking irony.'

'So what exactly do you suggest, Stace? That we abandon her? After all we have been through?'

John's face was a mix of many different emotions, but the most predominant was fear. Just plain fear for Julianna. What had happened to her? What was stopping her from making her way back? John knew she was too good an adventurer to merely forget directions. No, it had to something stopping her from coming back.

He wasn't even sure if she was alive. Stacy had her right to be angry. After a minute or so of contemplation, he thought if this had gone on for too long. No sooner had that thought crossed his mind than a voice cried out from a worker controlling the sensors.

'John, we found something! A hollow stone! Do you want to have it removed?'

John looked at his watch. Just five minutes left for the authorities to arrive.

'No. I don't think there is enough time. Stop the work. But do me a favor and mark that stone with something. We will excavate there tomorrow.'

Saying so, John walked toward the stone. It certainly looked old, no doubt about that. However, the edges were smoothly curved and almost as if done recently.

Bending forward, he touched the stone. The way the rock was positioned, and the hollow sound it made when John knocked on it, indicated that there was something beyond it.

In a light whisper, almost caressing it, John asked,' What are you hiding behind you?'

A few meters away, Stacy watched John closely. And so did someone else.

ॐ ✦ ☪

Burning Flame was peering into the screen of his Apple macintosh, looking at what had popped up. Of course, back in his homeland even a handheld phone was a distant dream. However, He had ensured his carefully built relationships had given him transformative powers over his dreams, along with that near invincible status.

On his computer screen, was a list of search items that popped up when Parmanu was typed in the search engine that Burning Flame had on his laptop was unique though. He had designed it himself.

It showed not just conventional results, but also all possible connections with major governmental treatises. It naturally followed that his search engine came with hacking software. Inspired by the Turing test that tested an AI's ability to be human, his software was called the New Turing, or TNT for short. It also fits in with his explosive nature, but that was a fight for a different day.

His first hit was 'Parmanu- The Age of the Atoms.' Atoms?

Burning Flame was hooked. The click was imminent. Almost immediately, a page came into view with the domain name reading ParmanuGuru. The layout of the page was decorated with sages and astronomers of lore, like Aryabhatta, Banabhutta, Madhava and more.

An interesting side note was attached to the page, which said that the Gregory Leibnitz series had actually been proven much earlier by Madhava, an Indian mathematician. As he read on, he realized that all of these past Indian minds had creativity of the highest order, and Burning Flame felt some respect creep up inside him.

Yet another link directed his attention to the fact that the value of pi was first discovered on the Indian subcontinent, and its application was found in the household item of the Tretagni, an altar consisting of three layers of a triangle, square and a circle respectively. The successlful amalgamation of all three layers required knowledge of the value of pi.

Aryabhatta was responsible for this feat, and a Sanskrit verse was his answer to the value of pi.

It read:

चतुराधिकं शतमष्टगुणं द्वाषष्टिस्तथा सहस्त्राणाम्।
अयुतद्वयस्य विष्कम्भस्य आसन्त्रौ वृत्तपरिणाहः ॥

Translated, it read:

Add 4 to 100, multiply by eight and add to 62,000. This is approximately the circumference of a circle whose diameter is 20,000.

Doing so gave the exact value of pi and was incredibly reliable. All this was blowing Burning Flame's mind, and he found these truths almost impossible to believe.

While he was delving into the wonders of Ancient India, Daniel was furiously dialing numbers, trying to call the Burning Flame, as he was the only one who could possibly get him out of this incredible mess, he found himself in.

Burning Flame saw the phone ring. He smiled and picked it up.

'Daniel?'

'Brother, something terrible has happened. I have been truly fucked over.'

At this point, Burning Flame knew that he was being for real.

'Listen. Take a deep breath and tell me what has happened.'

'Okay. I don't know how the fuck this happened, considering the precaution I took, but...

'Vilanova has been hacked.'

CHAPTER 14

Nasser called out to the French tourists he was now in charge of.

'Mademoiselle, monsieur, over here please!'

The couple, busy taking photos of Petra's entrance, turned around. Petra, in accordance with the rules of UNESCO, was now a protected site. Attracting about twelve million people a year, Jordan's pride was Petra. Other countries had already ratified this jewel, sending in teams of archaeologists for excavation and restoration. That is why, at the entrance, flying together at the gates, are the flags of many countries whose people stepped foot in Petra to study it.

Petra was bridging gaps and bringing people together. It's just like its glory days.

The couple, a burly man Jacques and his wife, Pauline now followed their guide as he led them inside the gate into a huge open market. Following the trail, they came to a stop in front of a huge board showing the different trails one could take in Petra.

'Madame, Monsieur, over here we can see the different trails of Petra. There is the kings trail, ministers trail and so on. But all these start from the basic trail up to Al Khwazneh.'

'Al Khwazneh? What is that?'

'Al Khwazneh refers to a treasury in Arabic. But I'll tell you more when we get there.'

Jacques peered at the various sites marked on the board.

'Sweet Jesus! Are there so many sites here?'

'Yes, Monsieur. Petra has just Al Khwazneh in its pictures, but the real beauties are hidden deep inside. Often, there is more than what meets the eye,' said Nasser.

'Alright, let's move on then,' said Pauline, rubbing her hands in suppressed excitement.

Nasser led them through the souk, and they turned left to see.

A massive valley. A footpath had been made, and beside it roads for one of the famous horse-rides to be done. They walked along the path, all the while reveling in the sights on both sides of the eye.

On their right, Nasser first stopped at the rock formations.' See, monsieur, these rocks are far too well-cut to have been made naturally. Nature does not get such a steep gradient.'

Click. Another photo for Pauline's camera.

Next, they kept walking until the starters really showed up. An inscription on a piece of rock. There were two lines of writing on it. One was the ancient Nabatiyan language, and the other was Greek.

'This stone helped us understand the Nabatiyan language better than ever before. As I often put it, this is our Rosetta Stone,' Nasser proclaimed, drawing comparison to the stone that helped decipher the Egyptian hieroglyphics.

Moving along, they turned yet again to the left. Now, buildings started to come into view. Jacques and Pauline were amazed at how huge the structures were, and the fact that they had all been carved out of rock was amazing. Nasser looked at their bewildered faces with a wry smile of satisfaction.

'These are the outskirts. Let me just warn you: there is much, much more. Get ready to be completely blown away. Nabatiyan technology was incredibly advanced and ahead of its time. These people thought like nobody else. And that is why they survived for so long.'

Jacques merely nodded.

Nasser gestured them forward, and they went on and stopped again at a bridge. On the right side, one could see a huge tunnel constructed and a huge canal almost underneath the bridge.

Turning to his guests, Nasser had a question.

'My friends, we begin here. Our tour begins now. But before I go on, let me start with the simplest of questions. How did Petra come into being? How did they achieve such a feat? What was the secret of the Nabatiyans that enabled them to caravan route from Aswan in Egypt all the way to Palestine and the Holy Land?'

'My friends, this tour is a quest. A quest to find out the real reason for the end of the Nabatiyans.'

Jacques smirked.

'All of this seems really weird to me, judging by the fact that very little trade happened in the Arabian region, a mere sliver of the trade that happened in Europe at the time. The Europeans were the most progressive bunch of the time, were they not? So it seems but natural.'

'Is it? I don't think so, Monsieur. This seems like the propaganda of the West. The highest exchange of goods, tradable's and other stuff took place in Arabia and Indian subcontinent. Not just goods, but knowledge was exchanged here,' he said, pointing his fingers downward.

Pauline clearly had a different view, and she wanted it clarified.

'Alright then, leave the trading. Why did they build this tunnel? I mean, it's a desert. It's obviously mostly barren land. So what was the point?'

'Right Madame. However, you have to understand that the sight you see today is not the same as when the Nabatiyans inhabited this place. The surroundings were vastly different. Lush green forests and clear running water. Nobody just built a city, there had to be factors influencing such an important decision.'

'Hmm. So what was the tunnel used for then?'

'Okay. So I need you to go back in time now, madame. Back to a golden age. Clear flowing rivers across the horizon. The Nabatiyans, as engineers, were skilled and innovative, and their city would have been damaged by the incessant flooding of the river during the rainy season had it not been for their ingenuity. This tunnel. What does it do? It was simply a diversion channel for the water to go away from the city. The design also ensured a kind of moat-like structure for a layer of protection around the city.'

'The bridge then. Built for commuters?'

'Yes, of course. How else would they have got in?'

Nasser suddenly straightened up.

"Okay, friends. Now, we start our quest. But remember, this is a World Heritage site. So, no littering, please," he said in jest, and the French couple let out a giggle.

They walked about a kilometer down a slope that led to a gorge. The gorge was massive and absolutely gargantuan. It seemed as if an entire landmass had been broken down and formed this … place.

But Pauline suddenly felt something creep up her body. Fear? The sight of the gorge had made her take a step back. Was there something happening that wasn't supposed to?

'Jacques will everything be alright?' she asked him quietly, lest Nasser hear her worries.

However, Jacques was too busy admiring the gorge to notice her question.

He should have listened.

ഔ✦ങ

The council should have come to a decision a long time ago. Anxtila hated the long, drawn-out discussion that the heads had. Always such a bore. Better to finish it off quickly and make do with it.

This was the fourth day of the meeting since the mistake had happened. There was no possibility for anybody to know how far the British had progressed. And the Incas made it a point to always stay a few steps ahead. Information was the ultimate power.

Secretly, Anxtila also had another, deeper desire in his mind. He secretly wanted to leave this mockery of a place and go back to the land that was rightfully his. Vietnam wasn't his home, and he could feel it.

Every day, it coursed through his blood as the thoughts of his homeland became a distant heartbeat whose presence was becoming fainter with each passing day. If the council had been in the Holy Land, the decision could have been entirely his. But they were outside territory.

He turned his bejeweled head to face the elders who were bickering on about the ethics of killing a messenger and some with the option of creating a new outfit.

Anxtila couldn't take it anymore.

'Quit it!' he shouted.

'What is wrong with you all? Can't you make one decision in time? Some of you are fighting about ethics, some of you are engrossed in your imagination, and some seem disconnected from the world. IS THIS YOUR DISCUSSION?'

The silence in the hall spoke powerfully.

'Fine. By royal order, the decision to make is mine. For far too long we have stood and watched as our homeland is ripped to shreds in the name of tourism and excavation. People are holidaying and lounging on the stones of our ancestor's hard work. Enough! It is time we win back our land.'

The crowd assembled was shocked at this last sentence.

The war commander of the High Council spoke up, bowing low in obeisance all the while.

'My Lord, what do you suggest? Do we fight our way in? But we are hardly an army of 100. Moreover, it's been years since we took to arms.'

'Who said we were going to fight? Besides, where fighting doesn't work, deceit will,' said Anxtila, and at this, it felt like even the air had come to a standstill.

'You want to fool your way in?'

'Yes. We have followed the rules long enough. It is time we broke some of them.'

ജ✦ര

Julianna stood still; the feeling of awe written all over her face. She had come down the staircase, feeling the stones as she passed them. Each stone had its own story to tell. This find alone was worth a fortune! Not just in monetary terms but also in the knowledge that could be gained through this goldmine of information.

It was true that the Incans had the most extensive road systems in the ancient world. Julianna was now facing a small underground room, where a palanquin, entirely of gold and silver, with the rods to hold it up made of bronze, lay at rest. On its front, a huge picture of the face of the King, the great Manco Inca, was plastered.

The first ever recovered face of Manco Inca.

Julianna gazed at the high cheekbones, aquiline nose, and slit-like eyes stamped onto a rounded face that reminded her of The Tibetan People.

Out of nowhere, instinct flooded her, and she pressed the very tip of the face's nose. She did not know how she knew, but his touch proved decisive. The palanquin swung around its place, revealing a previously well-concealed door that looked royal in appearance. It was done up in a monochrome black-and-white pattern, and a circle in the center was made with alternating gold and lapis lazuli slips. It seemed like the love of lapis lazuli that the Incans had never abated.

Moving toward the door, Julianna tried the most obvious thing and pushed it. She did it slowly at first, not wanting to damage such an antique ornament, but it did not budge. She applied a bit more force to it, but only a slight crack appeared.

Deciding to leave her skepticism aside, she took a step back and executed a perfect scissor kick on the door. Bam! It burst open, and a simple space with a stairway leading up came into being.

Relishing the prospect of higher ground, she made her way up the stairs, one at a time. After a few hundred or so steps, the gradient of the ascent began to change, and she saw the ground kind of even out, becoming flatter. A few hundred more, and she saw a light pulsating and glittering. A few hundred more, and it came into view.

There was a rectangular sheet formed by a pulsating mass of a green substance that was almost identical to the trapdoor that Julianna had studied about, which the Incans used to capture robbers who attempted to steal their famed treasure. Only that this one seemed to be...hovering, almost?

Feeling some dread, Julianna decided to push forward and went through to see… a hole. On it was something in Arabic:

الإمارات العربية المتحدة

She had learned Arabic as part of her language classes in her History Major, but all that knowledge deserted her as she realized that she was staring upwards at a manhole cover.

She moved her entire body against the cover and pushed it upwards. After some effort, she was able to push hard enough to make it bob upwards and slip out.

Sunlight streamed in.

Sensing the exposed space, she quickly slipped out and found herself on a sidewalk. Standing up, her gaze took her to the imposing buildings on the left-hand side, all high rises. In the foreground, a rail track was visible over her head. She turned right.

She didn't expect in the slightest what she saw. A signboard for Johnny Rockets greeted her, followed by the green of a Mermaid. Starbucks. puzzled to the absolute core at what part of Peru had Johnny Rockets, she then saw another signboard written in Arabic.

Her translation skills kicked in. She read the signboard and… no. It couldn't be.

She saw a man clad in a suit walking hurriedly in her direction. As he passed her, she posed the dreaded question to the man.

'Excuse me, sir, but where am I?'

The man stopped, gave her a long, hard stare, and then looked at the open manhole cover.

'Look, ma'am. Whatever this is, I don't have time for it. Let me go.'

'No, no, please! Tell me where I am!'

The man shook his head and started moving even as the words left his mouth.

'Dubai, of course.'

CHAPTER 15

Back at Raw headquarters, the team quickly gained some leads and added more and more information to the Sooraj file.

The first lead they had managed to crack was the National Crime Records Bureau. Two hits had emerged when a facial recognition trace was run on the software. One had been imprisoned in a Bangalore jail for money laundering and creation of fraudulent accounts to try and coax buyers to part with their online money.

Not their man.

Yet, the other hit was interesting. Known as Michael Mwongo, which was a fake name (the traces had been done), he had tried to hack into the CBI special investigations servers, specifically searching for a file numbered 22- BJCK-1176. He was African, of Nigerian descent.

Seemed a bit weird to hack into servers for just one file, yes? But no. this one was different.

This was the file that the Indian Government kept safe, away from people and their knowledge, lest it ever come out into the open.

This was the file on Operation Smiling Buddha. The Pokhran nuclear tests.

Previously conceived as impossible to achieve, the Indira Gandhi- led Congress government made the tests a success with financial help and this task was specifically taken by Mrs. Gandhi herself.

He had been sentenced to a minimum of 14 years behind bars in the dreaded Tihar Jail, but he had managed to get out thanks to some very thrifty key stealing.

The prison had made a mistake with its primitive lock and key mechanism, and Mwongo had taken the opportunity, as well as the upper hand.

He was now untraceable.

On closer analysis of the record files and the photo stills from the video of their agent, one could notice that Mwongo had shaved his head off and had developed a thick handlebar mustache, which managed to physically alter him, but the computer didn't make a mistake and gave them a 99.6 per cent match.

Madhav smiled and looked at Sunil.

'That's all there is. He is African, Nigerian, and he is a techie. That's what I could get.

'No, Madhav. This is more than enough info. Hafeez has been working on getting us some geographical co-ordinates of the place,' said Sunil.

And soon enough, a voice shouted from the other end of the room, 'Done! At last.

Sunil turned and walked over to him.

'What did you find?'

'Look, the transponder had a geo-indicator, but it had been damaged by the hypoderm. There were string values, though, that remained out of order. Reordering them took an entire day, but in the end, only one set of geographical co-ordinates made any sense. I typed it in, I got something but I'm not sure it's possible, Sunil,' said Hafeez.

'Not possible? Why is that?'

'No more computer work is possible. This place, I mean, we have got to go there ourselves.'

Sunil peered at the screen.

'Wait, they said something about Africa, right? What the fuck is this?'

The name that flashed on the screen:

Reykjavik, Iceland.

The specialists bickered. The electricians stared aimlessly. The servants dozed off. There was utterly no progress being made in retrieving the contents of Vilanova until Preziyan came up to the maintenance section and screamed a string of swear words that would have made his mother have a heart attack all over again. Workers scurried away, and work was moving.

On the other hand, Daniel clutched the phone tightly as the encrypted call now found itself being picked up at the General Secretary's Office.

'Hello?'

'All the Duma hails, hail the Duma. I need some help, Secretary, and I need it fast, said Daniel, defeat echoing through the phone.

'What exactly happened, Dan?' only the General Secretary had the guts to call him Dan. Anybody else would have got their head smashed in if they ever did try to address him as such.

'Vilanova has been hacked, and I need some searches done on the official servers.'

'What type of searches?'

'Names. One, actually. Garibaldini. Francesco Garibaldini. I need every possible evidence of anything that associates him and the Russian Federation. Send it to me by 5:30 pm at most. All details are in the usual encrypt. Thanks.'

The situation would have been comical, a don asking for the help of a government, but it was different. The national security of Russia was threatened, potentially. When it was a question of Mother Russia's safety, everybody was one and the same.

'Why Dan? Why do you need it?'

The question came over the phone, and so Daniel couldn't quite figure out the authoritarian tone of the speaker.

'Contacts, Secretary. I need him because he is useful to us. I don't think you would like to know more. Think of him as another Troboyan, will you? Ah! That reminds me. That package I told you about. Did you receive it?'

The Secretary stared at the body bag sitting in front of him.

'Yes, I did.'

'Good. Now it's your chance to send me mine.'

'I don't know what you're doing, Dan, but good luck.'

'Luck? Luck is for suckers. Trust me, and all will be well.'

The Secretary did trust Dan. Implicitly.

'And what rules are you proposing to break, my Lord?'

Anxtila looked around.

'Who dared to ask me that question? Who was that?'

A small hand rose up.

His eyes followed down to find the High Chief of war, as the black sheep.

'Why Huitzi? Do you really think we should be as subservient as we were before?'

The chief was deeply insulted, but he let it be.

Insulting? Yes. Huitzipochtli, or Huitzi, was the Aztec God of war. Abd calling a High Chief by his Aztec counterpart's name suggested one of two things.

Either the chief was an Aztec impostor to the Incan empire, or the chief had decided to swap loyalties. One had infiltration as the crime, the other had treason. Therefore, it was but a given that no Incan, especially a High Chief, would ever align with the Aztecs. Why would they? They Incans had everything. Even if, for some reason, they did swap loyalties, they had no need to advertise it.

The offense was punishable by death, especially if attributed to a High Chief. It was most definitely a swift execution and, hence, was a significant accusation. But Anxtila was the Sapa Inca. You had to tuck your tails in.

Anxtila realized what he said and immediately ceded ground.

'Chief, I apologize. All I am saying is we have been far too lenient. Let us listen to an idea I have just made. It is to send four central spies to Macchu Picchu, accompanied by two along the old Royal Minister's passageway.'

The chiefs were about to shout something in unison, but Anxtila rushed on.

'They will inspect the main platforms of Macchu Picchu, and one will be on the Cay Paccha platform's watch-house. We need to judge what damage they have done to understand their power. Then we attack.'

The astrological chief of the Inca, the Sun Priest Tanamambo, spoke up.

'Sapa Inca, our question is simple. How does one use the Royal Minister's passageway? That was broke down in the rebellion, yes?'

The rebellion the Sun priest spoke of was a small rebellion that happened during Sapa Atahualpa's reign. His decision to welcome Pizzaro, the conquistador from Spain, as a God was not received well, and that led to the formation of a conspiracy plot.

However, the Incans were builders, and their skills did not lie in killing, unlike their Aztec counterparts. And so they failed. But they had destroyed the Passagewat during a brawl with the King's royal guard and broke the mortar that held it together. It was this history that everybody in Tawantinsuyu, the Land of Four Corners, believed.

Anxtila merely smiled.

'You think so?' he said and pushed a lever on his throne.

The audience watched in amazement as His throne lifted up and swiveled sideways to reveal yet another trapdoor.

This one was…. weird, to say the least, with a skull made of glittering green jade fastened on its fore and symbols of Incan danger written all around it.

Pointing at the trapdoor, Anxtila said,' I built this. I never meant to use it, but it provides a safe passage to Macchu Picchu. You enter into the Hall of the Dead on the other side.'

The crowd couldn't believe it. The chief of war felt the words stumbling from his mouth.

'The Hall of the Dead! But then this door… this thing is.'

'Yes. This is the Passage of the Royal Death.'

கை✦ை

John watched the men drill through the rock he had marked.

The readings had been fine, but John still had the nagging feeling that there was another variable in this equation, that one variable which couldn't afford to be neglected.

The variable in question was now making its way on all fours, slowly circling the perimeter of the excavation site, its jet-black skin glistening in the Sun. Its emerald eyes focused on John; it stood still, muscles tense, ready to strike. There was hardly about twenty-five feet separating the two.

And yet, John remained unaware. He had gone on with the drilling and finally created a hole big enough for someone to go through it.

'Thank you, guys. You have been a great help, but I think I can take it from here.'

'Where do you think you are going, John?' came Stacy's voice.

'Uh, sorry, Stace! But I'm going in,' he said and popped inside momentarily before coming back out.

'Wait, does anybody have a flashlight?' he asked. They gave him one, and he jumped back inside. Stacy, shaking her head, followed him in.

No sooner had they jumped inside than the hole seemed to cave in, covering itself up. The two now found themselves in a sort of alley. Just as the flashlight switched on, John and Stacy could only hear the screams of the people as they were being eaten to death. Their wails echoed through the rocks, and the duo could not believe the lifeline they had just received. And there was nothing they could do to help. It was done.

The panther had attacked.

CHAPTER 16

Jacques and Pauline now walk through the gorge as Nasser explains the significance of the rock formations to them.

'You see, the denudation of the soil cover in this area led to the formation of this beautiful gorge that we are walking through. See the rock formations? Various gradients of red, yellow, orange, and black contrast each other to create a startling image.'

Pauline had noticed something. The rock had been cut into, forming a long chain like a mini canal that extended on for as long as the eye could see.

'What are those canals? What are they used for?' she asked. Nasser stopped and turned to look at what she was pointing at.

'Ah! Yes, Madame. Good observation. I was about to come to that. Remember when I told you how Petra was 5000 years ago? Yeah, so the rainwater used to be collected. It used to rain, didn't it? So it was forced through these channels, where it would slowly move down to the city of Petra.'

Jacques had another question.

'But what if they couldn't control the speed of the water? Water moves faster if it's flowing down, right?'

'Yes, Monsieur! But that is where Nabatiyan's minds were put to work. They thought ahead and built small drain swamps along the way. So the water would pool around and automatically slow down.'

Now, a faint click-clack of horses was heard as Nasser pushed them to the side.

'Over here! Monsieur! Madame! The carts are coming through.'

And sure enough, a cart came up, carrying two other tourists who had come to bask in the Nabatiyan glory.

As they walked for the next ten minutes, Nasser didn't speak. He was experienced in this business, and often, it was best to let the tourists absorb the place for themselves. There wasn't any point if it was him who did all the talking all the time.

They passed a place where a kind of God had been sculpted out of the rock. When asked about it, Nasser had merely said that the travelers coming here needed to feel like it was an auspicious yet comfortable place. So, to make them feel like this was their own place, God statues had been erected for them to pray.

The next question came after 5 minutes of a photo session with some amazing rock formations.

'Nasser, Uh…. How come the roads are half-paved?'

He looked down.

"You see these stones, Monsieur? That was the original pathway built by the Nabatiyans. The other part is a reconstruction done by UNESCO. If you ask me, though, I will say that the reconstruction takes away from the worn-down beauty of the past."

Jacques nodded in assent.

They headed on until a sharp right showed up. Nasser stopped the two and asked them to close their eyes, and Onoy opened them when he asked them to.

"Right. Friends, now we need to imagine something. Imagine the world from the sea of. Start your gaze downwards at the stone. Absorb the bright cream to the gray, and then slowly, very slowly move up each of the rock. Red, then yellow, then orange. Absorb the contrast and the mixing between the. Slowly move up to the tip of the gorge at the top, the very tip. See the sunrise hit the top and slowly flank its way down."

"Done? Now, look upon the sky, the ocean of blue. See the vex it creates of making the world look all topsy-turvy? Slowly move your gaze to the right, my friends, and move it from the top and then slowly downwards. Feel the aesthetics hit you as you gaze on…"

Jacques and Pauline were lost for words.

'That is…'

'Yes, Al Khwazneh. The treasury.'

ॐ ✦ ௸

Burning Flame looked at the mélange of information that was occupying his computer screen. He had gotten through to Daniel's pre-damage login page and had managed to get a hold of the codes that had been previously entered.

His desk was already full, crammed with a model of a new experimental light-aluminum rocket and a new weightless smart glass that transmitted real-time feed into a server along with information that one could pick up on when on a task. Again, inbuilt with a listening device with a range of about six meters from the stirrup of the wearer's ears.

Oh, and his food.

Burning Flame loved his breakfasts. He truly believed that culinary appeal was an incredibly effective way to a person's heart. The right mixture of ingredients, coupled with the right cooking style, was sure to produce a masterpiece. According to him, breakfasts provided the best opportunities for it to be showcased.

Today's dish was moussaka. It was essentially a dish of minced lamb and aubergines but Burning Flame had added his own garnishes. A bit of chili powder there, a smattering of seasonings and just a touch of olive oil. Nothing overdone.

But of course, drinks had to be there on the side. Today was Pulke. A Mexican alcoholic drink fashioned from the cactus; it was said that three small cups of this drink without adulteration could get you teetering on the brink of death. So, it is a Mexican death fiasco combined with a Greek masterpiece. Perfect start to the day.

The information that Burning Flame had retrieved revealed that the hacker had indeed tried to perpetrate the computer to give up its databases. Luckily, Vilanova, at the very least, had a failsafe for its databases. The Russians did not like to lose their upper hand, at least when it came to gathering information.

Three particular bits of coding stood out, though.

One: the coordinate virus had initially been planted as a bomber virus, but the virus could miraculously think for itself and had adapted its design to become a Trojan horse.

Two: the hacker had clearly wanted to keep out intruders, so he had built a wall of passwords, with firewalls making rings of defense and, as a jocose mockery of the Mafia, a fucking captcha.

The third bit of code was what Burning Flame was the most excited about. There was a small misalignment between two bytes of coding that could be exploited if one could insert the exact value that was missing from the code. Once typed in, the entire system could be debugged. Easier said than done. However, Burning Flame thought Daniel's men could handle it.

'Hello? Daniel? Good news, brother.'

'Yes! Finally. Tell me. Have we fixed Vilanova?' he asked with a heavy layer of concern.

'No. but I have found something. A misalignment. I will send you the exact placements now, but you have got to figure out the values yourself, okay? I think your men can handle it.'

Daniel did not need more. He always knew when Burning Flame was referring to his busy schedule.

'I understand. Thank you for everything.'

'Okay.'

As Burning Flame put the phone down, he thought about the progress his neighboring continents were making technologically. Hacking into Vilanova was supposedly impossible, but now it had been done. Impossible was nothing. Were they getting ahead of him? No. He could never let them be. But for now, food.

He tucked in, and felt the rich flavor hit him. However, a long 5000 kilometers away, Divyesh did not know what hit him as he fell to the ground, unconscious. His last memory was of a person, a young man, about seventeen years old, clad in a black jean and yellow shirt, balling his fists. And then, nothing.

֍ ✦ ֎

Johannes stared at the huge 55-inch TV set made by Bravia that he had bought last year. He had bought it, along with the other gifts to himself, as a result of the huge sum of money that had flown into his Cayman Islands account. He remembered the day of that terrific deal. That deal, which had improved his financial status, almost quadrupled it to include him in the who's who community.

It all started with one shared passion. Football. He remembered the game as well, an English Premier League game. Manchester City versus Manchester United. The Manchester derby. At Old Trafford. He remembered the meeting in the VIP lounge.

He was there, sipping a glass of champagne, a plate of the most heavenly black forest in front of him. Johannes remembered the nervousness he had felt when he had seen the man. Moving slowly, he had a sharp intake of breath when he realized that the man had noticed him.

'Come on, boy, and sit here,' he had said.

And so he had sat down, all the while noticing the cut of his suit tailored by the ever-impeccable Armani fashion house. It must have cost a small fortune.

They had talked business even as Manchester City hammered United, and their striker Kun Aguero made sure the Old Trafford pitch was nothing but a razed mass of hopes and dreams with some grassy patches in between. He had told him of a new jet that was in conception. It was modeled on the Tupolov-144, a Russian Jet whose western counterpart was the world-famous Concorde.

It was to be able to seat up to 160 passengers, which is small for a commercial flight, but it made up for the lack of passengers with its speed, hitting a maximum of Mach 3.6. They wanted to bring back the feeling of breaking the sound barrier. It was aimed to be sustainable, with reusable plastic bags being used to meet the plastic demands in the interior creation. Also, it would run on a relatively newer technology. Hydrogen cells.

Johannes remembered his question.

'What should I do?'

The man had merely given him a slip with the details of a Credit Suisse bank account written on it. He had asked him to create an account in some tax haven, like Mauritius or the Bahamas. Johannes chose the Cayman Islands.

"Using the account I gave you, transfer 80 million Swiss francs to your account. It will be your money, for your use and your use only," he instructed.

He had noted the surprise on Johannes' face.

"In the meantime, I want you to build me a missile. Yes. A missile. Something unique and different. Also, it is something that can be used privately. I don't want any high-end gizmo shit. Just a normal, predatory, old school missile that has a range of over 3000 miles. Oh, and the modes of deployment must not only be limited to land but should also include air and sea. The money you transfer is an advance fee. Once the job is complete, you will receive another 80 million francs. Good luck."

And with that, he had walked out of the lounge, leaving Johannes to his thoughts.

Now, he understood the influence that the rich have on the poor's beliefs. He realized the power that the man contained within him. A mere mention of his name sent shivers down the aviation industry's spine. There was nothing he couldn't make or destroy. An aviation fanatic's wildest fantasy, getting on his wrong side, could land you very far away, both from yourself and others.

This was Prys Danckinson.

Chapter 17

Dubai? Really? Of all the places she had faced on this treacherous journey, Dubai was the least expected and definitely the one she was least prepared for.

Was this some kind of sick joke? She had come so far. What could possibly have been the connection between Peru and now Dubai?

All this and more crossed her mind as she sat in the waiting area of the Dubai Metro station that she had stumbled upon. She looked at the board with a map of the routes covered. It showed that her station was called Burj Khalifa/Dubai Mall. Looking out of the window, she slowly pressed rewind in her brain with the visuals of the events that had unfolded.

First, she had walked all the way to the nearest police station she could find. It was a smart police station, she found out. Which meant there were no actual policemen! It was just a Robocop that rolled up to her, displaying a smile. She had typed in her problem, and it was but natural that her 'problem' received special attention. She was confronted by the Lt. General of the Dubai Police, Murshad Ali.

Murshad had flat-out refused to believe her story, but yet again, Downing Street came to her aid and gave her some much-needed identification. It was this highly unusual interaction that had led to her being granted a special five-day permission to stay until somebody from the British government came to pick her up or a flight arrangement was made.

She looked at the Dubai Mall in all its brick-and-cement glory, proudly displaying Cartier and Givenchy banners on its front. It has been listed in the Guinness Book of World Records as the largest mall by area.

Beside it is a modern wonder of the world, the Burj Khalifa. The massive tower stood in all its gleaming glass exterior, as the building played host to a range of high-class apartments, offices and the 5-star Armani Hotel.

828 meters in height, the Burj had initially been named Burj Dubai. However, on its inaugural day, the Sheikh of Dubai, HH Sheikh Mohammed bin Rashid Al Maktoum, named it in honor of the president of the UAE and the Sheikh of Abu Dhabi, HH Sheikh Khalifa bin Zayed Al Nahyan.

In front of the Burj Khalifa was the Dubai Fountain. Known popularly as the dancing fountain, for its showers of water that were irregularly timed to make it look like it was swaying from side to side, these three things formed a sort of trinity that visitors around the world flew in to see.

Julianna then thought about the planning it would have taken and the visionary thinking at its helm. How far, just how far, were these people willing to bet on the future and work in the present? In essence, Dubai also followed a very simple strategy that had catapulted this tiny city into fame. In whatever they did, they had to be the only one or to be number one. This concept was seen in the structures like Palm Jumeirah and the World Islands that were being built.

Roughly 60 years ago, the discovery of oil, the black gold, completely changed the trajectory of this lesser-known country. A nifty calculation of oil exporting had led to the amassing of a massive fortune. But there was always the issue of battling time. This could not run on forever. Oil was a fossil fuel, and fossil duels eventually get exhausted.

Again, foresight proved to be their saving grace. They used the money to build structures, parks, offices, and amusement-themed cities. In layman's terms, they turned Dubai completely, converting it from an oil-based economy to a tourism-based economy. The funds had to be allocated to ensure Dubai's long-term survival as a city.

From a business perspective, Dubai has become a tax-free economy. More and more business houses flew in, enticed by this idea of a financial oasis, and had allowed for some much-needed foreign investment.

Over time, Dubai began to live up to its name of 'The Pearl of the Gulf.' Today, it stood not just as a transit hub, connecting west to east, but rather as its own attraction at the epicenter of the world's geography.

Julianna suddenly felt very angry. She realized she hadn't eaten properly in days! It was a miracle she had managed to hold on for this long. She immediately stood up and got out of the station, walking toward the Johnny Rockets restaurant she had seen.

Upon entering the restaurant, she immediately felt a sense of relief. In some weird way, multinational food chains had that knack of making you feel in your element. As she sat on the stool after ordering a large fry and a double cheeseburger, her phone beeped. Julianna had lost her phone while clambering in that crazy cave, but the police had graciously given her another phone for temporary use. Even the numbers on the sim were provided by the police. She knew it was a way for them to monitor and potentially tap conversations. That being said, she did not have a choice. She glanced at the phone. It showed one new message. She opened the message to find something that almost made her lose her balance.

An attachment of a photo. A photo of John and Stacy getting into a hole in the ground, the very same one she had got into. And below it, just three words. Three words that she did not need to think hard for to understand the implications.

It read: Into the labyrinth.

॰◆॰

Divyesh came into consciousness as the scaffolding around his eyes had been removed. He slowly started to regain vision as he blinked several times, trying to make sense of his surroundings.

Night had fallen in Copenhagen. Normally, Denmark had a very active nightlife, but surprisingly, this was quiet. It must be a suburban area on the outskirts of the city center.

He used his sense of hearing to get more information as his eyes adjusted to the blinking light that had just been switched on. There was a clang of metal and a constant buzzing of machinery. Also, oddly, he could hear the chirping and night-calls of birds. A loading or docking area, perhaps?

Slowly, something came into view. A face. He tried to move his hands to try to touch and feel it, but he couldn't. His arms had been tied strongly to the chair. High grade industrial strength ropes had been used for the purpose.

His vision cleared; he now could notice the finer details of the face. Undoubtedly a female. Indian, by the fact that there was a bindi on her forehead, and married, judging by the tilak, bright red, extending into the top of her head.

She spoke first and with a very heavy Irish accent.

'Good! You're awake. Divyesh, so I need you to do some work for me. You are from the CBI, right? So you are just right for the job.'

She suddenly stopped, and a smile came up on her face, reflecting her apparent joy.

'Oh, how rude of me! I forgot to introduce myself. I am Bindhya Wade, and I am the head of this small group of rebels who are fighting against the Indian Government.'

Divyesh merely looked around the room, staring at the eclectic mix of nationalities that made up this group. He counted off about 200 personnel as an approximate, with an index of about seventeen nationalities at face value, the predominant one being Indians.

His mouth, thankfully, wasn't covered, and he could ask the questions that came to his mind.

'Why me? And what the hell are your objectives?' is what he could ask as the thoughts finally began to come in a stream.

He got a guffaw in response.

'That's it? That's all you got. Tch. I'm disappointed, Divyesh. Is this the mettle of the CBI?'

'I'm not with the CBI; I'm with RAW, you chutiya!' Divyesh shouted out. This woman was really pissing him off.

At the insult, the Indians who understood had flung out knives and axes and the others, seeing the reaction, proceeded to do the same.

Bindhya turned to them.

'Go back, people! Stay away. This is strictly between me and him.'

'Divyesh. Let's not lie right now, hmm? You say you are with RAW, but that's not really the case, is it? Why are you here? Yeah, let's start with that. Why are you really here?'

Divyesh was contemplating whether to lie or not when the lady did something really unusual. She slapped herself again and again.

'Why can't you make him tell him, Bindhya? What is wrong with you?'

Her nut has definitely rusted, to say the least, thought Divyesh. What on earth was going on here? Just to make sure that some normalcy was returned to this meeting of sorts, he decided to open up just a tiny bit.

'I'm here for the expo.'

He found himself being held roughly by the collar as Bindhya looked directly into his eyes.

'Don't you dare, Divyesh? Don't you fucking dare? We know you are here for the conference. You are my lucky goat, Divyesh. You will be the one to execute my plan at the Inter-governmental conference. I will make sure this is an experience the Indians back there will never forget!'

At the port of Istanbul, a huge yacht was docked. She was officially christened the 'Pearl Red' for her ability to be the eye-catcher among the various other boats owned by a myriad of high-profile individuals.

This particular baby, however, was owned by the person now standing on its edge, clutching a glass with the magic of Johnnie Walker occupying the space in it. Jorge Janismat, the Turkish sea billionaire.

The yacht did a lot of jobs, and it had been decked out for various functions. Today, however, it was playing the role of a venue for another one of Jorge's well-known booze parties. It was normally accompanied by the popular trio of girls, whiskey, and drugs, with a higher concentration of the first and last.

The yacht was now divided into three segments based on the three floors it had for each activity. The topmost was for the partying, the middle for the drugs and the lowest level was for exploring the pleasures of the flesh.

Jansimat turned his head to see two absolutely stunning women looking casually at him. One was a blonde, and the other was a brunette. He walked over to them.

'You girls looking like you need some help,' his thick Arab accent pronounced.

The blonde adjusted her form-hugging backless dress that was cut above the navel in a touch of daredevilry. Janismat immediately liked it.

The brunette, on the other hand, went for a more flowing dress with a double skirt that seemed to have the effect of provocatively stretching up her dress every time she bent. It was super titillating, especially for him.

When asked what their names were, they responded with Tressa and Lulia, respectively. Janismat moved closer and placed his head in between both of their shoulders. The girls were on a whiskey-induced run, and they nibbled at his ears. He turned to the blonde first, as he had felt this strange, unexplainable connection to her in the beginning. Their lips drew closer and finally met. The brunette licked the nape of his neck. They interchanged positions next and kissed with an intense passion that only reflected their drug usage.

Finally, he extricated himself and pointed to the stairs.

'Care to join me downstairs?'

෩✦ಜ

CHAPTER 18

'Who would want to go to Reykjavik?' came Sahil's voice. He had been silent for so long and finally decided to speak up.

'What do you mean, who would want to go? Someone has to go, right?'

'It is either one of us or all of us.'

Raghav looked at the stare-off between Hafeez and Sahil and immediately burst out into laughter.

'What happened? Why are you rolling on the floor like a madman?' asked Sahil, while looking at the others and twirling his fingers around the side of his head in the universal symbol of lunacy.

'No! Haha…I mean, look at your face!' he shouted and resumed his laughing fit.

Now, both Hafeez and Sahil pitched in.

'Stop it now, will you? The idiot thinks our faces are a piece of shit.'

Almost immediately, Raghav stood back up and the smile was gone. He said in a serious voice, 'Guys, we do not have time for fights, alright? So let us get this decided by a vote. People that are for just one person operating this, raise your hands now.'

It was even, divided with Sahil, Raghav, and Sunil all in for the idea, and Hafeez, Trix and Madhav in favor of everybody going as a team rather than relying in one individual.

'Right. It is a tie. We move on to a vote decided by a coin toss then.'

Suddenly, Trix jumped in.

'Wait! One more member is still left.'

'Who?'

'Divyesh. Have you forgotten so soon?'

Raghav's shoes now held his fascination as he peered down at them.

'right, then let us call up Divyesh. They, I mean the Ministry, told me they didn't change his number, apparently,' said Sunil.

'Okay then. Let's call him.'

Sunil fished out his phone and searched his contacts for Divyesh.

David, Danckinson, Divyesh, Dushyanth….

'There! Before Dushyanth,' said Hafeez, looking into Sunil's phone.

Sunil turned in shock.

'Did you just read my contact list?'

'Yes, I did. Who is this Danckinson?'

Sunil's body immediately tightened up at the mention of the name. He could see the dawn of realization on Sahil's face as he understood the person being referred to. This truth was slowly spread to the other people present as well.

'Uh. just a friend. We met at an airshow somewhere. He said he owned some shares in companies and wanted to talk business, but I refused at that time. He gave me his number for future reference; he said as he coolly finished his fabricated story. But he knew that the suspicion would still remain.

"Oh. Okay. Go ahead and call him," replied Hafeez.

Sunil tapped on Divyesh's icon and felt the rings. One…. two. Three. Someone picked it up on the third ring.

'Hello?' said a shrill female voice.

Sunil covered the phone and whispered to his colleagues. 'It's a woman.'

Amid snickering, he asked his next question.

'Who are you? And why do you have Divyesh's phone?'

'Ooo! Interrogation. You must be the friends from Raw, in that case.'

'You know who we are? Then you know what we are capable of. Where is Divyesh?'

'Never in your wildest dreams am I telling you. Now listen to what I want. Two million US dollars, cash, left on the doorstep of Divyesh's house. At 4 o clock sharp on the next Friday, that is the day after tomorrow. No police, no military presence, no funny tricks. Just Sunil and the money.'

'You know Sunil?' he said as he turned to look at him. Sunil was, naturally, dumbfounded.

"Ey! Does this feel like a meet-and-greet session to you, Mister? Quit asking me stupid questions. Just do exactly what I tell you to do, and there is a slim chance you will get to see Divyesh again. As for now, goodbye."

As Sunil put down the phone, he heard the woman say something else.

'Hello? Hello?'

'Yeah, I forgot to tell you something.'

'What?'

'Jai Hind.'

The duo stared at the façade, open-mouthed. It was beautiful, kind of a miracle that just popped out of the rock. There were pillars, four of them to be precise, and it was done on two floors. The first was simple, with just the pillars, a main chamber and two side chambers that were dead ends. It was put there to improve the overall effect.

It was the second floor, however, that really caught one's attention. A sculpture of a jar was placed on a pedestal, surrounded entirely by hollowed structures that were supposed to have been filled with the Guardian angles of Petra. However, they had been destroyed.

This jar was once surrounded by a rumor. It was apparently filled with gold coins, and if one could break it, they would have all the gold fall down. But it was empty.

On top of the two extreme pillars sat the states of eagles. The eagles were believed to symbolize power, and the finer details of the pillars revealed the unmistakable Roman influence on the architecture.

All along the side of the façade, there were marks. Mostly, these were by people who had made attempts to reach the jar in order to put some truth to the rumor and improve their financial conditions drastically in the process.

But all in all, the façade was a symbol of strength and the integrity of the Nabatiyan empire. Far from establishing a kingdom, the façade ensured their glory was etched in the pages of history for eternity.

Jacques now noted that there had been grills placed on the ground, a few meters from Al Khwazneh. He turned to Nasser, who was busy on Facebook.

'Nasser! You have Wi-Fi here?' exclaimed Jacques.

Pauline turned in surprise.

'You do? Why didn't you tell us?'

Nasser smiled.

"Of course, we have Wi-Fi at a few dedicated hotspots. We aren't a primitive bunch, you know. And yeah, it is free," he said, much to the delight of the tourists.

After they had been logged on to the Internet, Jacques asked the question.

'Why are there grills placed over there? What are they covering?

'Hush!' said Nasser and pulled them both over to one side.

'What I am about to tell you now as it is a little secret. You see, I am an archaeologist, and I have done excavations here as well.'

'Wow!' came Jacques's appreciative voice.

'Yes, and I was part of the expedition that went down there. Do you know what we found? An underground area! This whole façade was just a lie when the entire treasure was underneath.'

'What was in it?'

'Oh, it was a tomb of some form of royalty. But never mind that. Are you done taking your photos?'

Jacques and Pauline took one more selfie together before turning back toward Nasser.

Pauline suddenly became morose.

'Is this it? Is this in its entirety, Petra? That's all there is?'

'Madam, this is a World Heritage site. There is always more than what meets the eye. And what is in front of you often pales in comparison to what is behind you.

'Excuse me!' Pauline exclaimed, miffed at the inappropriateness of the sudden statement.

'Uh… I meant Al Khwazneh, Madame. Now, would you please mind walking with me. I want you to do the finding part yourself. Only then will you be able to appreciate it completely.'

And they walked. As they neared the turn, Nasser stopped them and said, Don't talk at all when you see it. No words at all.

Curiously, they moved on.

As the turn came, they first noticed the shops. As they moved forward, it hit them. Hard. They found themselves staring at something otherworldly. For the third time that day, they were at a loss for words.

Nasser tiptoed up behind them and whispered into their ears.

'This is the real jewel in our crown. The city of Petra.'

🕾◆℞

Prys Dickinson, aviation King, now sat on his airplane-themed sofa as he watched CNN. He was wearing his bathrobe, which had the proud emblem of the Kempinski on it. He never forgot to have something aircraft-themed in his room, and Kempinski had chosen the sofa.

He was in the Kempinski Dubai, a grand 5-star hotel that boasted close proximity to the Mall of the Emirates and Ski Dubai, a snow world inside the mall that was eternally covered in snow and even had its very own penguins!

He looked at the ornate Rado timepiece that was on the wall. The time read 8:50. Perfect time for breakfast.

He went to his wardrobe and came out dressed in Balenciaga from head to toe. Prerogatives of the rich.

In the lift, he pressed the button that said zero. There were precisely 16 floors between him and the ground.

As the lift started, a beautiful rendition of Uptown Up by Maceo Parker started to play, and Prys was transported into his own personalized dreamland, dominated by aircraft in the sky. Ah, to be a human and feel like a bird.

A sudden 'ting!' of the lift brought him right back to the present.

The lift had stopped on the seventh floor.

It opened to reveal a lady, dressed in a cream jumpsuit. She stepped in and possessed an elegant gait. Looking at the button for the ground floor, she saw it was pressed and relaxed. The lift closed.

Prys never did like silence much. He wasn't really used to it. In school, his classes used to be horrendously noisy. People would shout and scream at the top of their voices, and he had come to love it. Habits that stick couldn't really be removed that easily.

Even now, noisy boardroom fights and talks and busy markets were his sort of thing. A yoga or meditation class, however? Not so much. If given a chance, he would live his life out at the Stock Exchange.

Breaking the silence, he finally said, with a weirdly lopsided grin, 'Hi!'

The lady turned toward him.

'Hi! How are you?'

'I'm much better now that I've met you, my lady,' he said, smiling.

She gave a little chuckle.

'What's your name?'

She smiled and replied almost immediately.

'What's yours?'

'Danckinson. Prys Danckinson.'

A look of recognition shot across her face. Prys was pleased. This was the reaction he had been expecting, and he got it.

'Oh my God? Are you Prys? The aviation maestro? It is an absolute honor to meet you sir.'

'Yes, yes, but enough of that. I've told you, my name. It's time for you to return the favor.'

'Of course, of course. My name is Julianna. Julianna Herbert.'

ഇ✦ൽ

John moved forward, all the time trying to figure out any damn clue that Julianna had ever crossed the same path. It was almost as if the labyrinth was teasing him, getting him to move further into its depths so that it could play.

Stacy, on the other hand, was surprisingly unmoved by the situation. She had been quite the diplomat, and during her time with the British houses of parliament, she had answered many questions and addressed various tough possibilities. She had conditioned herself to analyze and inspect and nothing more than that. It was obvious to her that their own chances of survival were getting bleaker by the second, but John had blind faith. And blind faith had power, immense power that made the believer impervious to anything else.

As John contemplated his next five steps, Stacy stopped him.

'John! Enough. Can't you see? This whole thing is a sham, and it has been that way from the start. Any clue-finding will take hours, maybe days' worth of work. We don't have days. Why do you persist in your actions?'

As John turned to look at her, Stacy could have sworn that she saw a flash of gold run through John's eyes, but just for a second. John merely smiled.

'He has put His faith in us, and we shall put our faith in Him. He will lead to our freedom.'

Stacy was completely taken aback.

He had now turned to divinity! Oh wow, she thought.

As these very thoughts swam across her mind, Stacy suddenly glimpsed light. She saw it, pulsating and wavering like there was wind about. They moved closer, only to find out an object on the floor of the endless hallway.

A phone.

As John held the phone, he gently pressed the power button of the iPhone. Instantly, a lock screen came into view. Both of them knew that unlocking the phone wouldn't be necessary.

From the phone's screen, Julianna Herbert's face popped up, smiling at them.

CHAPTER 19

Setting that little incident with Vilanova aside, Burning Flame could now concentrate on the task he had originally given himself: Parmanu.

The page he had been viewing listed 'Parmanu' or atoms and 'Manu' or molecules as being the early discoveries of Indian physicists. Apparently, all these discoveries had come at an age when Westernization was non-existent, and the western world was trying to walk on two feet!

Indians had a complex and intimate understanding of nature, and their curiosity led to their discovery of the fundamentals of matter. Of late, many people have attempted to rediscover the past in order to reinvent the future. Connecting Ancient India's text and physics, a very famous quote had been uttered by Robert Oppenheimer at the detonation of the first atomic bomb. 'I am the God of death,' or something like that.

Interestingly, Oppenheimer had pored over the ancient Indian texts like the Vedas and Upanishads in particular during the course of his discovery of the atom bomb.

Only one logical conclusion came to Burning Flame's mind from this small paragraph, in regard to what the man had said. The Indians were building some kind of bomb. But it couldn't possibly be that simple, could it? Besides, the Indians already had their own bombs. Pokhran had ensured that.

What was it then?

Burning Flame disliked failures. So he exited the page and checked the next thing that came up. 'Parmanu, the story of Pokhran,' was next. For a moment, his blood rose as he read the excerpt, returning to normal as he realized it was just a movie. Although one is starring John Abraham. Burning Flame absolutely adored the guy for two reasons. He was buff, and he was badass. Glistening abs and bulging muscles was his religion, although he rarely practiced.

He exited the page, although with a heavy heart. He had no way of knowing that exactly 24 hours from then, he would meet somebody called John. Just not the John he wanted.

ജ ✦ ൽ

Johannes was back at Yale. Today's lecture was by some obscure historian, albeit on a very intriguing and interesting topic, Secrets of the Indian Rise. Johannes strode with the others into the beautifully built halls in order to listen to him speak. They didn't have to wait for long.

A man strode up to the dais, walking with an air of purpose like he knew the job and he was there for it. Oh, and he looked nothing like a historian.

His fashion game seemed to be strong, by the look of his feet being snugly kept inside loafers that looked suspiciously like limited edition Jimmy Choos. Dressed in a Versace suit, his silk pants held together by a belt that spelled Bulgari, this man was a perfect representation of what Beverly Hills stood for.

Taking a hold of the mic, he started.

'Good afternoon people. my name is David Sentosa.' Johannes was on the front rows, two rows behind the VIP's and the line of security. Awed expressions clung to people's faces as they caught a glimpse of the man who was universally recognized as the man behind the Unknown Man affair.

What was it all about? The Nine Unknown Men were reportedly the world's first secret society, formed during Ashoka's reign, and had dabbled in the dark arts of the time, or in other words, advanced sciences.

According to popular history, the Nine Unknowns were in possession of a single object. The object rotated between each of the members for security reasons, and it was rumored that this object commanded influence of dizzying proportions. Influence in the scientific world. It enabled some of the brightest and greatest minds of India to unravel the mysteries of science and make progress by leaps and bounds to make Bharat the most technologically advanced place in the ancient world.

However, when it came to what the object was, not one clue could be found. The only way they knew about this object's very existence was through an obscure 5th century text that David had managed to source. The archaic Sanskrit conveyed in startling clarity that there was a base for this building of glittering knowledge. India. And to be more specific, the period of the Mauryan Empire.

David's book touched upon some really mind-boggling possibilities, but as far as Johannes remembered, only one stood out. David, in all his adventurous zeal, had proclaimed through his book that the Indians were, in fact, not the independent thinkers that the world had perceived. That is exactly what he was explaining in his speech.

'In fact, throughout my long research career, I found, nah, discovered that the Indians were influenced. I thought at first, how did Aryabhatta, Madhava or even Katyayan get all these theories and formulas? How could they be so advanced, particularly when they were starting from scratch? So, I summarized that some kind of raw material should have been there for them to begin with. Turns out I was right,' David said.

And then he paused.

All Johannes managed was a weak nod. It didn't matter if he had already read it a thousand times. The revelation still retained its brain-shattering nature.

"I found that the Indians had been contacted by another civilization long before their meteoric rise. A civilization is older and much more deep-rooted at the time. The crumble of those in power and the breaking up of its unified legacy led to a surviving few managing to smuggle its old glory into India, giving the land of the Ganga and the Indus their secret wealth - knowledge."

My friends, India had been the foster home for the Chavin culture, and they were the forefathers of none other than… the Incans.'

ॐ ✦ ॐ

Anxtila had retired back to his private chamber. Just calling it a room would not have been an appropriate description. It was huge, and many stories were built underneath the real surface line. Decorated with the likings of the personage residing in it. Also, the Vietnamese government had listed it as a mere cottage. Anxtila recalled a passage he had once heard during his Incan schooling:

"Nobody sees straight; everybody sees none"

"All the riches lie before your eyes"

"You need not two, but only one"

"But jealousy curtains, draped over like ice."

It was so true. Humans had blinded themselves. Anxtila wasn't blind, though. He had, a long while ago, hit upon a beautiful ten letter word that proved to be the defining link of him, separating him from his ancestors. Technology.

Long ago, the Incans ruled the sphere of maths, science, and technology. Now, in the present age, a bunch of paper-pushing western scientists decided what was considered breakthrough technology. Ridiculous!

Who said technology was specific? The Incans proved the world wrong over and over again. The walls, the history it held, it spoke a thousand words.

But all that swept out of his mind as he recalled an even better vison of himself. The key to his success in the Inca circle was not due to influence, it was due to knowledge.

The Incans valued knowledge and intelligence highly, and he had ensured nobody, absolutely nobody, could question his authority. All that would not have been possible without his greatest discovery, the collective years of effort paying off in a single find.

He had found it. The legend, the myth, the belief. The greatest gift to the Incans by Viracocha himself. Inca rule was favored by the Gods, his ancestors had reasoned, and had found this miraculously at the foot of God's statue at his grand temple in Cuzco. It contained the direction they needed desperately, the right formula. In essence, it was a sort of Rosetta Stone but of knowledge itself.

The crumbling of the empire, as well as its fortresses, led it to be taken out of Peru for eternity to be used to bring to power a newer, stronger force that would rise on the blood, sweat and tears of the Incan knowledge. The ancients had a strict code, and the code specified the emergencies to be taken in case of an attack. One of them was the safety of the secret. It also specified the qualities necessary to possess the secret. Only one civilization fit. The Indians.

Why didn't the Incas have another, more secure backup? Egyptians, Chinese, Roman…. So many empires? Why were they so late? Even Babylonia wasn't as far away. So why the delay?

Again, this was another question to which no answer was available. One could only look to the stars and gaze at the faces of the ancients, glancing down at their handiwork.

Coming back to it, did Anxtila still have it within him? The secret? The Peruvian 'Rosetta?' Alas, no. The US war had given him sufficient reason to change the ownership of it to another person, a person so unknown to the Incans that it almost guaranteed it would never be touched.

All Anxtila ever knew about that person was that he worked for the Chavin's second home: India. No trace of a name, or a face. If memory served him right, they had never even met. The object in question had been smuggled over to India through various US bases until it reached the Indian Ocean. And then, the Indians had taken care of the rest.

Suddenly, a single word struck him. He had remembered it, quite unusually. One of his aides, who had been trusted with trying to find out its location, had given him a vague answer but which he knew was connected, in some way, to India.

He remembered RAW.

What did RAW have that could possibly have been so important to the Incans? A stone, or a sculpture of some sort?

Nope. It was just a scroll.

એ ✦ ૦૨

Anxtila was back at his throne. Today was the day they made the descent. With torches in their hand and hearts aflutter, they went into the tunnel and began the journey.

It went on for an hour.

At last, they came across a fork. The way split!

'Which way should we go?' thundered Anxtila. General voices said left. And left they went. Slowly but surely, the end began to come into view.

Triumphant that no one was expecting them, they pushed on.

They should have chosen the 'right' path.

CHAPTER 20

Julianna was clasped by absolute, uncontrollable fear for the umpteenth time. How much more did she have to endure? First the labyrinth, then Dubai, and now this?

Trembling, she went over to contacts and immediately phoned Murshad Ali's personal phone number. She placed the phone to her ear, all the while thinking just what the Lt. general's reaction to such a piece of news would be. That, too, something about their phones? A breach of their network security? A huge, huge problem indeed.

She heard the rings. One…. two…… three. On the third ring, he picked up.

'Hello? Julianna?'

For once, Julianna was overjoyed to hear the thick draws of his Arabic-accented English.

"Yes, Mr. Murshad. It's me, Julianna. I have news. Terrible news," she said and narrated the message and the photo that had arrived on her phone. No, their phone that she was temporarily using.

Murshad was understandably ticked off.

'What the hell is that?! Who dared to break into the Dubai servers? And that, too, a line as secure as this? No, no, this is no ordinary work. This would need hackers of the highest caliber, and even then, it's a stretch. Who the fuck could it be?'

Murshad realized quickly enough that the best way to figure out the problem was to personally examine the phone. She requested him to come to the Mall of the Emirates, which was quite close to her, and wait for a passenger drone.

Dubai had tested their so-called flying taxis with flying, and they were well on their way to being fully operational. Julianna was about to hang up the phone when Murshad asked another important question.

'Uh, Julianna? When did you receive this, um, picture?'

She told him the truth. It was quite a while ago.

'Well, why didn't you come to us earlier?' was the obvious response she expected. And he didn't disappoint. Apologizing profusely, she kept down the phone. She obviously didn't have time. What was she going to do?

Far, far away, in an unknown part of Africa, covered in dense foliage, under a hut, a man started laughing. Hacking that shit had been easy enough. These servers were supposed to keep everybody out, but it was impossible to crack. But not for him. He was extraordinary. He was out of this world.

He was the Burning Flame.

ജ ✦ ൽ

He took it all at once. She took it one at a time. Nasser watched with nascent satisfaction as he saw both Jacques and Pauline change facial expressions by the second.

As he walked by the main street, Nasser was now in full control. He felt at home.

'This is the main street now, folks. We will now move on to either the King's trail or the common man's trail. Which one do you want?'

Jacques was already up and rolling.

'King's trail, s'il te plait! I'm feeling like one today myself! What say you, Pauline?' Which trail holds your fancy?'

For once, Pauline did not disagree at all.

Nasser perked up.

'Tres bien! That's decided, then. The King's trail it is. I'll be honest, I was going to take you on that trail first anyways,' he said with a jovial smirk.

They moved quickly to the right, where the road forked in two.

They had to climb through a lot on this route. Up they went, trudging through rocks and the sweltering heat. On the way, Nasser briefed them on the sights that could be seen while traversing this route.

'We, on this route, will get to see many kings and royals' tombs. Some are huge, and some are in ruins, but you will see. Oh, and there is also the Rainbow Palace.'

'The Rainbow Palace? What is that?'

'Oh, you'll see. Patience!'

'Oh, come on!' said Pauline, and sulked a little bit.

Smiling, Nasser led them up to some beautiful vantage points en route. Pictures were taken in a frenzy, absorbing the beautiful moments into the contents of an SD card.

Finally, the trio huffed and puffed their way up, although Nasser showed some endurance by repeatedly refusing a drink of water. Only the first part of their journey was done; they came to a halt upon a huge stone. Nasser, on the other hand, did not seem to have lost even an ounce of energy.

'Monsieur! Madame! Come on, this is the view. Look at this! Isn't this beautiful?!'

Jacques and Pauline were treated to a panoramic view of the main street, with the highlight being the Amphitheater in the middle. The Nabatiyan people were really ethereal builders.

After a quick break, they resumed their trek. This time, though, the journey was shorter. They took a bend in the road and found a natural path, turning right. Go straight and turn right, the rocks seemed to say. And that's precisely what they did.

It was like an angle, jutting out of the rock face. The first tomb had revealed itself.

Nasser allowed them a few moments with the camera and then took them inside. There, he showed them the interiors.

'You see the rock interface here? There is a close contact between different types of rocks. And you know, the rock is so old, and its structural integrity tends to weaken……' he murmured off, muttering about geology, more to himself than to the tourists.

Jacques, meanwhile, had found something else to question Nasser about.

'Why is it black on the walls? Is it…. Soot?'

Nasser nodded.

'Yes, it is. Up until the site became a UNESCO protected one, people lived here. Bedouins. A lot of them. They would burn fires here at night, to beat the extreme cold, and the residue was left on the walls. Defacement, really, but what could we do? They weren't al knowledgeable about this place,' sighed Nasser.

Pauline still hadn't let go of her request.

'Alright then, if you're done with your geology, can we go see the Rainbow Palace now, please? I genuinely can't wait!'

'Alright, Madame, your way it is. On we go. Please exit carefully and lower your head. The roof is a little small.'

And out they went.

'Madame, the next turn is a little bit more interesting. You have got to go down the slope and then back up it again. Understood?'

Pauline's 'huh?' was left unnoticed. They turned and walked back down a path. They almost immediately found another road and started climbing up it. Once they were almost at the top, something huge caught their eye.

It was a huge well, or collecting duct, with a single inlet in the center.

'It was used to collect rainwater in those days. They had a surprisingly efficient canal system that ensured everybody got water.'

And saying so, they took the final step of the climb, and as if out of nowhere, a huge façade just came into view.

It was impossible to know how they hadn't noticed it at first!

'You can now see why it's called the Rainbow Palace,' said Nasser.

'I sure can,' said Pauline and gaped at the structure.

In terms of carving, it was as normal and huge as any other royal façade. However, what set this one apart was the. Streaks of blue, red, orange along with brown were all visible.

'The various rock formations undergo some processes, and this is what we get. A stunning sample of nature's beauty.'

Saying so, he took them inside.

There wasn't much except the same wisps of various. However, on closer inspection, there was a kind of stone door on the floor.

Pauline was suddenly gripped by the same sense of fear when she had first laid eyes upon the valley. This time, she expressed it to Nasser.

'Nasser? Uh… I mean, is it okay to feel a bit scared now?'

Nasser turned around.

"Yes, of course. Claustrophobia is completely natural. Don't you worry? You will be fine."

And then they heard it.

Thud. Thud. Thud.

'Hmm... that is unnatural...' said Nasser, looking down at the floor.

At the same time, Pauline's phone pinged, indicating a message. She opened it to see she had received a photo from an unknown number.

Opening the attachment, it showed a photo of some kind of dark, underground place and two people that Pauline had never seen before.

Below the photo was a message that read:

"Food for the beast. John and Stacy."

ෆ✦ಜ

The team at RAW was completely undecided on their next course of action. What do we do now? Was the question lingering in everybody's mind? As yet, no definite answers had been found to this question, so there was silence in the air.

Yet again, Hafeez broke the silence with a small voice.

'I don't know what is right or what is wrong at this point in time, but I do have an idea that we can use to try and get Divyesh back.'

'Go on,' said Madhav.

'And before I start, don't fucking skewer me if you find any mistakes.'

A loud 'OK' was heard from the team.

'So, we are getting a signal, even now, from the biochip in Divyesh's body. Are we not?'

'Affirmative, replied Sahil.

'And we have a good idea of where Divyesh was taken. Somewhere near the Rue de Straaten. So, essentially, we have a hit on the location, and also the biochip showing no signs of stress means he is still unharmed. I propose we take this to the mill because we are short on time.'

Mill, by the way, referred to the military.

'Also,' Hafeez continued, 'this is a diplomat since he was attending a conference. Technically, he has diplomatic immunity, so why not issue a government alert?'

Sunil immediately intervened.

'It's a huge process, and as you said, we are short on time. We need to take matters into our own hands without involving the government. Also, Sooraj should be kept on hold. Divyesh is far more important now.'

And Trix finally spoke up.

'Raghav?' she asked. He stood up and moved toward the group.

'What did you think the kidnapper would be like?'

'Hmm, judging by her tone, Brainwashed thoroughly but intelligent enough to see what's in it for her. Her comment, 'Jai Hind,' definitely suggests something Indian or an event of Indian cause or origin that had affected her. I'm thinking the family angle,' he ended.

Trix agreed.

"That could be the case. What say? Sunil, are you going to go and drop the money, or what?"

Hafeez smiled.

'Shouldn't we drop the money and then wait for her to pick it up?'

The group was confused. And they did not hesitate to express it.

'Hold on. I mean, Divyesh is the obvious priority. That money would lead us to him. It's just that she is too clever for that, from what I could gather about her. She would immediately find out any sort of tracing bug we lay on the bag. So…'

Madhav suddenly thought of something.

'What about we stick to old school? Counter blackmail. It is the tried and tested method, after all, is it not?'

'No Madhav, we need to find out who she is. We have no leverage, and even if we did, it is too risky to just fight this with words. No, this needs guns.'

Suddenly, realization dawned on him.

'Wait! Yeah, an army. That is what we need. No, not the Terminator kind,' he replied to glares from Trix.

'A digital one. In essence, we are going to let the money be propagated to their bank account. I mean, she is not keeping all that cash forever. She had to deposit it somewhere. When that transaction gets completed, a virus enables the money to be rerouted while having the account infected for details. How does that sound?'

'Ok, so we inform banks of the notes' serial number and flag accounts that get caught in the web. I like it. Who is going to do it? asked Madhav.

And the eyes that stared back at him were answer enough.

ॐ ✦ ॐ

Anxtila was ready. The day had come. They had walked up the path that had started all the way back in the throne room. They felt the path widen up, almost a gentle slope up several meters. Everyone felt the blood coursing through their veins.

'Brothers! This is our birthright! The right time for the Inca to be back to their glory has come! So march! March ON!' Anxtila shouted.

'Kawaschun Inca!' he cried.

'Sapa Inca kawaschun!' came the resounding shout. And they marched, beating the clubs on the ground as they moved forward.

Thud. Thud. Thud.

After an excruciating half hour or so, they came upon a wall. The head of the council looked up and examined the wall.

'This is the final barricade,' he whispered to Anxtila.

And Anxtila roared the message back to his comrades.

A posse of young men produced a battering ram, fashioned out of a metal with a ram-like protrusion, and upon Anxtila's commands of 'Maqay!' banged it upwards against the wall.

Everybody felt the ground shake.

More motivated than ever, they continued to beat against the wall, willing it to break. Finally, they broke through.

The rocks crumbled. They waited. Waited to get a glimpse of their long-lost land, taken unlawfully away from them. As the rocks broke and the wall above caved in and fell, the witnessed a sort of stone room appear in their sight. They looked, and they realized the markings weren't Incan. In fact, there was very little marking at all.

As the last of the rocks fell, Anxtila climbed up and gazed upon the room he found himself in, desperately looking for signs of the Incan royalty. But as soon as he looked straight ahead, he knew a major blunder had happened.

All that he could see were three people, two men and a wildly bewildered woman, staring back at him.

Pauline nudged Nasser. Nasser, still dumbstruck, beckoned with his head.

'Was this part of the tour?'

ଔ ✦ ଓ

End of part one.